**Max stiffened, squaring his wide shoulders, his handsome mouth flattening. If he did marry Tia as Andrew had urged him to do, no actual wedding would take place for months. Max refused to rush into anything. He liked structure, order, strategic planning. He didn't do impulse or invite disruption in any field and would never have scaled the heights he had without serious self-discipline.**

The limo drew up outside the brightly lit hotel. Max sprang out first and then disconcerted her by peeling off his suit jacket and draping it around her shoulders as she emerged from the car.

"Is that really necessary?" Tia inquired, reeling a little and struggling to find her balance in the ridiculous heels as the fresh air engulfed her.

"*Sì*... If you can turn *me* on this hard and fast when I'm striving to stay cool, I imagine other men will stare, too, and I am assuming you would prefer not to be stared at and lusted after," Max murmured in a raw undertone, astonishing her with that abrupt and unexpected admission. "On the other hand, if you enjoy being the center of male attention, give me my jacket back... It's entirely your decision."

*She* turned him on. Tia was exhilarated by that grated confession and clutched protectively at his jacket, reveling in the intimacy of the silk lining still warm from his skin and the faint evocative fragrance of his cologne that still clung to the fabric. She breathed that fragrance in like an addict. The attraction *was* mutual.

## Wedlocked!

*Conveniently wedded, passionately bedded!*

Whether there's a debt to be paid, a will
to be obeyed or a business to be saved...
she's got no choice but to say "I do!"

But these billionaire bridegrooms have
got another think coming if they imagine
marriage will be that easy...

Soon their convenient brides become
the objects of an *inconvenient* desire!

Find out what happens after the vows in:

*Expecting a Royal Scandal* by Caitlin Crews

*Wedded, Bedded, Betrayed* by Michelle Smart

*Trapped by Vialli's Vows* by Chantelle Shaw

*Baby of His Revenge* by Jennie Lucas

*A Diamond for Del Rio's Housekeeper*
by Susan Stephens

*Bound by His Desert Diamond* by Andie Brock

*Bride by Royal Decree* by Caitlin Crews

*Claimed for the De Carrillo Twins* by Abby Green

*The Desert King's Captive Bride* by Annie West

*The Sheikh's Bought Wife* by Sharon Kendrick

*Wedding Night with Her Enemy* by Melanie Milburne

Look out for more **Wedlocked!** stories coming soon!

*Lynne Graham*

# CLAIMED FOR THE LEONELLI LEGACY

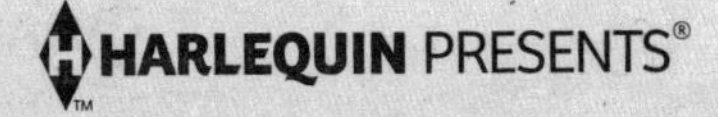

Recycling programs for this product may not exist in your area.

ISBN-13: 978-0-373-06101-3

Claimed for the Leonelli Legacy

First North American Publication 2017



This edition published by arrangement with Harlequin Books S.A.

For questions and comments about the quality of this book, please contact us at CustomerService@Harlequin.com.

**Printed in U.S.A.**

**Lynne Graham** was born in Northern Ireland and has been a keen romance reader since her teens. She is very happily married to an understanding husband who has learned to cook since she started to write! Her five children keep her on her toes. She has a very large dog who knocks everything over, a very small terrier who barks a lot and two cats. When time allows, Lynne is a keen gardener.

## Books by Lynne Graham

### Harlequin Presents

*Bought for the Greek's Revenge*
*The Sicilian's Stolen Son*
*Leonetti's Housekeeper Bride*
*The Secret His Mistress Carried*
*The Dimitrakos Proposition*

### *Brides for the Taking*

*The Desert King's Blackmailed Bride*
*The Italian's One-Night Baby*
*Sold for the Greek's Heir*

### *Christmas with a Tycoon*

*The Italian's Christmas Child*
*The Greek's Christmas Bride*

### *The Notorious Greeks*

*The Greek Demands His Heir*
*The Greek Commands His Mistress*

### *Bound by Gold*

*The Billionaire's Bridal Bargain*
*The Sheikh's Secret Babies*

Visit the Author Profile page at Harlequin.com for more titles.

In memory of all the great Mills & Boon authors
who went before me and inspired my stories.

# CHAPTER ONE

'IT'S A VERY big favour and I have no right to ask it of you,' Andrew Grayson admitted ruefully, angling his wheelchair closer to the fire, his pale worn face taut.

Max Leonelli, a multimillionaire financier at the age of twenty-eight, who had known Andrew since he first entered his household at the age of twelve, frowned. 'Anything,' he declared, without hesitation in making that pledge.

Andrew surveyed the younger man with quiet pride. It was way too late to admit that he should have married Max's aunt and adopted him. His housekeeper's nephew had come into his life as a homeless adolescent, traumatised, frightened and distrustful. No sign of those traits was to be seen in the powerful and sophisticated businessman Max had become.

Women, furthermore, were mad for Max. The beautiful boy with wounded eyes had grown into a striking man with olive-toned skin sheathing spectacular bone structure and a hard, challenging gaze. Max was tough and his humble beginnings and horrible childhood had merely made him tougher but he was also fiercely loyal. And since Andrew's failing health had removed him from the daily stresses of his international business empire, Max had been at the helm of it in firm control. While it had been Max's baptism of fire he had proved to be more than equal to the challenge.

'This goes *beyond* anything and you won't like it,' Andrew warned him.

Max was confused because Andrew usually came straight to the point. 'OK…'

Andrew breathed in, his breath rasping in his struggling lungs. 'I want you to marry my granddaughter.'

Black-lashed dark eyes flaring bright as topaz in the firelight, Max stared back at the older man in sheer bewildered disbelief. 'Your granddaughter lives in a convent in Brazil.'

'Yes and I want you to marry her. It's the only way I can protect her when I'm gone,' Andrew declared with conviction. 'I should have fought her father when he refused to let her visit me but up until last year I still hoped that Paul would come home and step into my shoes and I didn't want to alienate him. After all, she was *his* daughter, not mine. It was his right to decide how he wanted her raised.'

Max released his pent-up breath slowly. Marry a girl he had never met? A convent-bred female oddity who had not returned to the UK since she was born? It was an utterly extraordinary request but it was also the only serious sacrifice Andrew had ever asked of him and would inevitably be a *last* request because Andrew was dying. At that thought, Max's eyes burned as though he had got too close to the fire, his sleek, strong, bone structure tightening into disciplined rigidity because Andrew's quiet dignity demanded that restraint.

'Tia is all I have left, my only surviving blood relative,' Andrew reminded him heavily, his shadowed eyes veiling at the acknowledgement as he turned his greying head away, momentarily sidetracked by the grief of having lost both his sons.

Three years had passed since his elder son, Steven, had died childless, but it was only two months since Andrew had received word that his younger son, Paul, had succumbed to a sudden heart attack in Africa where he had been buried without fanfare and without ever properly mending fences with his estranged father. Tia was Paul's daughter, the result of his short-lived marriage to a Brazilian fashion model.

'She should have been made a part of our lives long ago,' Andrew sighed.

'Yes,' Max agreed, reflecting on what little he had learned about Tia's father, Paul. A generation younger than both of Andrew's sons, Max had only ever known Steven. Steven had worked for his father for years, a conscientious plodder who lacked initiative. Paul, so Max had been told, had been far brighter and more promising, but he had walked out of his job in his mid-thirties and gone off to become a missionary, severing his ties with his father and the business world and ultimately losing his wife in the process. On Paul's first posting to Brazil, his wife had gone off with another man, leaving her husband and her infant daughter behind her. Paul had dealt neatly with that unwelcome responsibility by placing the little girl in the care of the local nuns and continuing his travels to work with and preach to the poor in the world's most troubled places.

'Why would you want me to marry her?' Max asked gently.

Andrew groaned. 'Think about it, Max. She knows nothing about our world and she'll be a substantial heiress. It would be like throwing a newborn baby into a shark tank. She will desperately need someone to look after her and guide her until she finds her own feet.'

'She's not a child, Andrew,' Max pointed out wryly. 'She's…what? Twenty-one?'

'Almost twenty-two,' the older man conceded grudgingly. 'But she still needs a safe harbour until she can learn her way in this cut-throat world.'

'She may have grown up in the Amazon Basin but she may also be a great deal more current than you think,' Max argued.

'I doubt it and, while thousands of my employees depend on the stability of my companies, I'm not prepared to take that risk. I have a duty of care towards them as well. Tia will be a sitting duck for fortune hunters. I've been in contact with the Mother Superior at the convent. My biggest concern was that Tia ultimately intended to become a nun but apparently she has never expressed that wish.'

'So why is she still living in a convent in her twenties?' Max enquired with a faint edge of derision.

'I understand that she works there now. Don't judge her, Max. She's never known anything else. Paul was a very rigid man and frankly more than a little sexist in his outlook. He wanted a son. On his terms a daughter was simply a worry and a disappointment. He seemed obsessed with the idea of keeping her pure and safe from modern influences. I believe he hoped that with his encouragement she would eventually enter the novitiate.'

'But she hasn't.' Raking a long-fingered hand through his black tousled hair, Max strode restively across the room to help himself to a malt whiskey while wishing that he could not see Andrew's point of view.

As the Grayson heiress, Tia *would* be a target and Max knew what that felt like because he had been a target since he made his first million. He knew more than most about being wanted primarily for his wealth and the richer he became, the more he was stalked, pursued and flattered by women who would have been equally keen to catch him were he ugly and old.

'And I'm very fortunate that she hasn't because everything I worked all my life to achieve would be sold up and given to the convent if she were one of the sisters there,' Andrew pointed out ruefully. 'I owe my employees more than that. I would also like to meet her…'

'Of course you do.' Max compressed his wide sensual mouth. 'But I don't need to marry her to fulfil that wish.'

'It's unlike you to be so slow on the uptake,' Andrew murmured wryly as he frowned at the younger man with shadowed blue eyes. 'Obviously I want to leave everything to you and Tia together.'

*'Together?'* Max repeated in a stunned undertone.

'As a couple. If you marry Tia you become family and my empire will become absolutely yours. I know that, no matter what happens between you, when I am gone you will continue to look after her interests as well as your own. I *trust* you to do that,' Andrew completed with satisfaction. 'That's what's on the table, Max. This arrangement would greatly benefit you as well.'

Max stared back at him in shock for it had never once occurred to him that he would inherit anything from Andrew. 'You can't be serious…'

'I'm very serious,' Andrew assured him. 'I have already had my will redrafted to allow for that development.'

'You're prepared to try and bribe me into marrying her?' Max breathed in consternation.

'It's not a bribe. I prefer to call it a realistic incentive. After all, giving up your freedom would be a big sacrifice for you. I know that. I also appreciate that you have no current plans to marry and settle down,' Andrew stated grimly. 'And goodness knows what Tia will be like after the strange cloistered upbringing she's had. She certainly won't be like the sort of women you usually take out and about.'

Max stared down into his glass, reluctant to comment because he didn't usually take his women out and about, he simply took them to bed. He didn't do girlfriends and dates. He kept his affairs much looser than that, never offering flowers or explanations or exclusivity. That way there were no misunderstandings, no expectations and no dangerous routines or suggestion of permanency established. There was nothing complex about his attitude. He liked sex and he didn't need or want to commit to any woman to enjoy it.

'On the other hand, I can say upfront right now that I understand that this may be simply a starter marriage for you both. Isn't that what they call it these days? A *starter* marriage? You and Tia may not get on and one of you may eventually want your freedom. I'm not unreasonable. I have faith that you would do right by Tia even if you separate. That said, what do you have to lose?'

'You've given me a lot to think about. I can see you've considered this from every angle,' Max conceded, the smooth planes of his lean, strong face tight and unrevealing.

'And you haven't outright refused,' Andrew pointed out with satisfaction.

'You're assuming that Tia would be *willing* to marry me. That's a pretty big assumption.'

'Max, you've been romancing women since you were fourteen years old.'

Max winced. 'I don't do the romantic stuff and I'm not prepared to lie to her. I'll consider the idea. I can't promise more than that.'

'Time's ticking on,' Andrew reminded him heavily. 'I've told the Mother Superior that I'm ill and that you'll be flying out there to collect Tia and bring her back here. She was very protective of Tia, demanded a lot of details from me and a character reference for you.'

'Right,' Max sighed, a steel band of tension tightening round his head, that and the occasional nightmare the only hangover from his dysfunctional childhood. He got nasty migraines and he could feel the approach of an oncoming attack.

'Tia *could* be the love of your life,' Andrew remarked in an upbeat tone. 'Stop being such a pessimist.'

Having notified Andrew's live-in nurse that he was leaving his patient alone, Max mounted the stairs of the big house. *Love,* he thought with rampant incredulity. Only Andrew, the veteran of a long and happy marriage and a wife who had died long before Max's arrival, could talk so knowledgeably and confidently about love.

Max had never experienced love. His parents hadn't loved him and his Aunt Carina, Andrew's former housekeeper, who had given Max a home when he'd needed one, hadn't loved him either. Neither a sentimental nor child-hungry woman, Carina had done her duty by her dead sister's son, nothing more, nothing less. And bearing in mind his sordid childhood, Max didn't blame his aunt for her coldness. If he too struggled with memories of his dark past to the extent that he had never yet discussed it with anyone and hated even to think about it, how much harder must it have been for his mother's sister to feel any genuine warmth towards him? After all, nothing could ever change the reality that he would always be his father's son.

Even more pertinently, Max had good reason to distrust love and the damage it could do. He had become wildly infatuated with a girl in his teens and it had been a disaster. His supposed best friend at the time and the girl Max had loved had schemed against him, hoping to destroy him and cover their own sins. He had seen first-hand the harm that trusting and loving the wrong person could unleash.

So, no, Max didn't seek love in his life. Even so, he had dimly assumed that it would sneak up on him again some day and catch him when he wasn't protecting himself from its treacherous influence. But that hadn't happened either. He was entirely heart whole and rather ashamed that the women in his life were all but interchangeable, not one more memorable than the last. He went for identikit brunettes with a sexual confidence to equal his own. He didn't daydream about them, didn't miss them when they were absent, indeed he reckoned that they were purely a selfish means to an end. He gave them jewellery and they gave him sex and if he stopped to think about that exchange it left a nasty aftertaste in his mouth.

A wife, however, was something else entirely and the very concept of a wife brought Max out in a cold sweat. A wife would be around *all* the time, particularly a clingy, dependent one, who needed support.

Of course, he could say no...*couldn't* he?

Unfortunately, Max was ruled by two very strong drives. One was loyalty, the other an equally fierce streak of ambition. Andrew had presented him with the perfect package deal calculated to tempt. Andrew had been his mentor and the closest thing Max had ever had to a father. Everything that he had achieved he owed to Andrew, who had paid for the expensive education that had propelled Max and his razor-sharp wits straight into the heady realms of meteoric business success. Yes, Andrew had had motives of his own for that generosity, he conceded wryly, but that did not change the fact that Max had profited greatly from his support and advice. How could he possibly refuse to offer that same support to Andrew's last living relative?

In addition, Andrew had mentioned that all-encompassing word, *family*. Max would become family if he married Tia. The word, the very connotations of the word harboured a mysterious allure for Max that increased his discomfiture. All his life in one way or another Max had been an outsider. He had wanted to *belong* and he never really had—not within any group—because he was very much a self-made man. His dirt-poor repugnant background, which Max himself could never forget, kept him isolated in many ways. At his exclusive school the other pupils had been from privileged backgrounds and he had naturally kept his childhood miseries a secret for fear of being pitied. His birth family had not been a family in the normal sense of the word and Andrew's careless reference to Max becoming one of *his* small family had made much more of an impression on Max than the older man could ever have guessed.

The rain was torrential and like no rain Max had ever seen in his life. The downpour that had already reduced the road to a dangerous mud bath still bounced in shimmering noisy sheets off the windscreen and bonnet of the heavy-duty four-by-four he had hired to convey him from Belém to the Convent of Santa Josepha.

Through the flickering vehicle lights ahead he saw, not the established mining settlement he had dimly expected to see, but something more akin to a shanty town. On both sides of the road tumbledown buildings, shabby cabins and even tents stretched off in every direction. The view put him strongly in mind of a refugee camp. Meanwhile his driver continued to chatter in voluble streams, possibly explaining why so many people were braving such primitive conditions to live in the back of beyond, but Max understood only one word in ten because although he was fluent in several languages, sadly Portuguese was not one of them.

An ornamental bell tower loomed ahead and he sat forward, noting the dark outline of the extensive buildings rising behind a tall manicured hedge.

'*Estamos aquí*... We are here!' his driver proclaimed with an expansive wave of his hand as he stopped at a gated archway, shouting out of the window until an elderly man appeared and moved very slowly, his narrow shoulders bowed against the wind and rain to open the heavy wooden gates.

Max suppressed a sigh but, while he was weary after the unexpectedly onerous journey and his delayed arrival, he was far from bored. In fact Max's adrenalin was running at an all-time high and he sincerely hoped that a hot shower and a meal awaited him in the accommodation the Mother Superior had offered him for the night. Above all though he was incredibly impatient to meet Constancia Grayson and discover if Andrew's last wish was in any way viable.

Unaware of Max's arrival, Tia was swathed in a plastic rain poncho to deliver food on a battered tin lid to the mournful little dog sitting patiently waiting for her below the shrubs outside the doors of the chapel.

'Teddy,' Tia whispered guiltily, hurriedly looking around herself to check that she was unobserved before bending down to pet the little animal as he eagerly gobbled up the food she had brought.

Pets of any kind were forbidden at the convent. When human beings were going hungry, using precious resources to feed an animal that did not itself provide food was unacceptable. Tia told herself that she was using her own food and not taking from anyone else but Teddy's existence and her encouragement of his attachment to her weighed heavily on her conscience. For Teddy's sake she had done things that shamed her. She had *bribed* Bento, the old man who kept the gate, not to close the hole in the fence that Teddy used to enter the convent grounds. She had lied when Teddy had been seen in the playground and she had been questioned, and she was lying every time she smuggled food off her own plate to take outside and feed to him.

But Tia *loved* Teddy to distraction. Teddy was the only living thing who had ever felt like hers and just a glimpse of his little pointy tri-coloured face lifted her spirits and made her smile. Only what was going to happen to Teddy now that she was supposed to be travelling to England? But *would* that actually happen? After more than twenty years at the Convent of Santa Josepha, Tia couldn't imagine *ever* getting the opportunity to live another life in a different place. That seemed like a silly fantasy.

Why, after all, would her English grandfather suddenly decide he wanted her when he had ignored her existence for so many years? And now, worryingly,

Andrew Grayson's representative had failed to turn up to meet her. Mother Sancha had said the man's non-arrival was probably due to the bad weather but Tia remained unconvinced. Tia, after all, was very much accustomed to broken promises and dreams that didn't come true. How many times, after all, had her father visited and suggested that she might eventually be able to leave the convent to work with him? Only it had never happened. And over two years ago he had paid his last visit and had declared that it was time she became independent because he could no longer afford to contribute to her care. Once again he had suggested that she become a nun and when she had asked why she couldn't live with him and support him in his ministry he had bluntly told her that a young attractive girl would only be a hindrance to his work, and her safety a source of worry.

After her father's death the solicitor had explained that there was no money for her to inherit. Paul Grayson had gifted her his bible and left his savings to the missionary team he worked with.

Tia hadn't been the smallest bit surprised to be left out of her father's will. It had always been obvious to her that her father had no great fondness for her or even interest in her. Indeed, nobody knew better than Tia how it felt to be rejected and abandoned. Her mother had done it first and then her father had done it when he left her at the convent. He had then cut off her options by refusing to help her to pursue the further education that could have enabled her to become properly independent of both him and the convent. So, how could she possibly abandon Teddy?

Teddy *depended* on her. Her heart clenched at the image of Teddy trustingly continuing to visit long after she had gone only to find that there was no more food for him. How could she have been so selfish as to encourage his devotion? What had she been thinking of? What were the chances that he would miraculously find someone to give him a home? In two long years nobody had cared enough to do that while Tia had slowly transformed Teddy from a living skeleton to a bouncy little dog. Teddy had been abandoned too, probably by one of the miners chasing the gold rush, who had left again in disappointment when he failed to make a notable find and his money ran out. The prospectors regularly left women, children and animals behind them.

Hurrying back to her room in the convent guest quarters, Tia peeled off her poncho and hung it up. Her hair was damp and she undid her braids, brushing out her thick honey-blonde hair to let it dry loose. There was nothing for her to do now but go to bed and listen to the little radio one of the girls at the convent school had given her. Occasionally she came across magazines and books in the bins when she cleaned the school building and that helped her to stay in touch with the outside world. Although she earned a wage for her work, there was nothing much to buy within reach and she had been slowly accumulating savings at one stage, only that hadn't lasted in the face of women struggling to feed hungry children. She was a soft touch and unashamed of the fact, confident that she knew which women were the decent mothers, whom she could rely on to use her money to buy food rather than alcohol or drugs.

A knock sounded on her door and she opened it to find one of the sisters, there to tell her that Reverend Mother Sancha was waiting for her in her office.

'Your visitor has arrived,' Sister Mariana told her with a smile.

Tia hurriedly straightened her hair but there wasn't time to braid it again. Smoothing down her rumpled clothing, she breathed in deep and headed downstairs into the main convent building. Her grandfather's representative had arrived, she registered in genuine surprise. Did that mean that she was truly going to travel to England and the grandfather who hadn't seen her since she was a newborn baby?

'Tia is a very kind, affectionate and generous girl and she may impress you as being quiet,' the Mother Superior informed Max levelly. 'However, she can be stubborn, volatile in her emotions and rebellious. You will need to watch over her carefully. She will break rules that she disagrees with. At the moment she is feeding a dog she has adopted, which is not allowed, and she has no idea that I am aware of her behaviour.'

Max studied the calm, clear-eyed nun and reckoned that very little escaped her notice. 'She is not a child,' he asserted in gentle reproach.

'No, she is not,' the Reverend Mother agreed. 'But although she badly wants her independence I'm not sure that she could handle too much of it too soon.'

'I'll keep that in mind,' Max fielded, relieved to hear that Tia was imperfect and desired her independence. Somehow Andrew had given him a disturbing image of a pious young girl with high ideals, who would do no wrong, and he found the elderly nun's opinion of her character reassuring rather than off-putting.

And then the door opened and Max's mind went momentarily blank as a young woman of quite extraordinary beauty tumbled through the door spilling breathless apologies. A great mass of honey-blonde hair tumbled round a heart-shaped face, distinguished by high cheekbones, cornflower-blue eyes and a perfect pouty little mouth. Her skin was flawless. He breathed in deep and long, disconcerted and temporarily stuck for words, which was a quite unfamiliar experience for Max with a woman.

Tia stopped dead a few feet inside the door. In the lamplight, one glance at Max literally took her breath away. He had one of those almost Renaissance faces she had seen in illuminated manuscripts. Smooth bronze skin encased a sleek, stunning bone structure that framed a straight masculine nose, a wide sensual mouth and eyes as dark and rich as chocolate, fringed by dense black lashes. He. Was. Gorgeous. That reaction thrummed through Tia like a bolt of lightning and suddenly all she was conscious of was what she herself lacked. She had no make-up, no decent clothes. Her hands smoothed down over her skirt in a nervous, awkward gesture.

'Tia. This is Maximiliano Leonelli, whom your grandfather has sent in his stead,' Mother Sancha announced.

'You can call me Max.' Max relocated his tongue as he sprang upright and extended a lean brown hand in greeting.

'Tia…' Tia muttered almost inaudibly, barely touching his fingers and gazing up at him in surprise, for she was quite astonished by his height. He had to be well over six feet tall and she only passed five feet by two inches. The few men she met were usually smaller, much older and of stockier build and few of them were clean. Max in comparison was all lean, muscular power and energy, towering over her in a beautifully cut suit of fine dark grey cloth.

She had her grandfather's eyes, Max recognised while trying to fathom what she was wearing and what sort of shape was concealed beneath the frumpy long, gathered skirt and the worn peasant blouse with its faded decorative stitching. She was small in stature and either very thin or very tiny in proportion, her breasts barely visible in the loose smocked top, her slender hips no more prominent below the skirt. She wore stained espadrilles on her feet and for an instant Max was incensed by her poverty-stricken appearance, but he didn't know who to blame. Paul for being a lousy, neglectful father or Andrew for not trying harder to make his son put his daughter's needs first.

'You can show Mr Leonelli to his room and ensure he receives the meal I have ordered for him,' Mother Sancha suggested. 'You'll be leaving us tomorrow, Tia.'

Tia whirled back, her blue eyes very wide. 'Will I?'

'Yes,' Max confirmed.

The Compline bell for prayers peeled and Tia tensed.

'You are excused for this evening,' Mother Sancha told her. 'Mr Leonelli is not a practising Catholic.'

'But what about your soul?' Tia shot at Max in patent dismay.

'My soul gets by very well without attending mass,' Max told her smoothly. 'You'll have to accustom yourself to living a secular life.'

Catching the Mother Superior's warning shake of her head, Tia folded her lips, taken aback by the prospect of a grandfather who never attended mass either. Her father had said his father, her grandfather, lived in a godless world and it seemed on that score, at least, he had spoken the truth.

'I expect prayers are an inescapable part of life in a convent,' Max remarked as he accompanied her down the corridor.

'Yes.'

'Nobody will prevent you from attending services in England,' Max assured her thoughtfully. 'You will be free to make your own choices there.'

Tia nodded, a little breathless about the prospect of *having* such choices.

'What exactly does your job here entail?' Max asked as they mounted the stairs, noting that her golden hair tumbled as low as her waist, or to where he guessed her waist had to be since the tremendous amount of fabric she wore prevented any body definition from showing.

'Lots of different things. Every day I go where I'm needed. I bake, I clean, I work in the orphanage with the young children. I give English lessons to the girls in the school. Sometimes I go out in the community to work with the sisters.'

'The community looks like a refugee camp,' Max commented.

'There's been another gold rush. Someone found a tiny bit of gold and because of that miners flooded in from everywhere. Nothing's been found since, of course, so the fuss will die down and most of the prospectors will give up and move on somewhere more promising. Right now it's like the Wild West out there,' she told him with a rueful smile.

Max studied the perfect bow of her upper lip and the soft inviting fullness below, his body stirring, sexual imagery awakening that for the first time ever embarrassed him. He tensed defensively. And then argued with himself. To marry her he *had* to want her. He could not marry a woman he didn't find attractive. Why was he trying to stifle a natural physical reaction? Andrew's granddaughter was a classic, unspoilt, utterly natural beauty. Of course he was reacting.

Tia showed him into the room at the other end of the corridor from hers. 'There's only you, me and Sister Mariana up here, so it'll be quiet enough.'

Max elevated a fine ebony brow. 'Are nuns noisy?'

Tia cast down her eyes but not before he had seen the brightening leap of amusement in them. 'That would be telling...'

Max was entranced and he forced himself to study the room instead, unsurprised to see that it was as bare as a cell with an iron bedstead set below a large wooden crucifix and the absolute minimum of furniture, while cracked linoleum snapped beneath the soles of his hand-stitched leather shoes.

'The bathroom is opposite. Do you want to eat first?' she prompted, staring up at him, wondering how often he had to shave because black stubble already covered his strong jaw line. Her curiosity about him was intense. In fact dragging her attention from him was proving to be an incredible challenge.

'Yes...feed me,' Max teased, black lashes semi-screening his dark golden eyes as he gazed down at her, marvelling at the glow of her skin even below the stark unflattering light shed by the bare bulb above them. 'I'm hungry.'

'I'll take you down to the refectory.'

'And tell me about the dog,' Max suggested. 'I understand there *is* a dog.'

'Who told you about Teddy?' Tia gasped in horror. 'Oh, my goodness, Mother Sancha *knows*, doesn't she?'

'I would say that very little gets past that woman and of course she mentioned the dog. If you want to bring him back to England with you I will have to make arrangements to allow him to travel,' Max pointed out levelly.

Her heart-shaped face lit up with instantaneous joy. 'I can bring Teddy with me?' she cried in wonder. 'Are you sure?'

'Of course you can bring him, but he will probably have to spend some time in quarantine kennels before you can take him home with you again,' Max warned, mesmerised by the sheer brimming emotion that had flooded her formally still little face and glittered in her beautiful eyes. 'I'll have to check out the rules and regulations and organise it.'

'I can't believe I can just bring him like that,' Tia confided in amazement. 'Won't it cost a lot of money?'

'Your grandfather is a wealthy man and he wants you to be happy in England.'

'Oh, thank you, thank you…*thank you*!' Tia wrapped her arms round Max with enthusiasm and gave him a fierce hug of gratitude without even thinking about what she was doing.

For a split second, Max froze because he wasn't accustomed to being hugged, in fact could not recall *ever* being hugged by anybody, and that acknowledgement in the face of her enthusiasm made him feel uncomfortable and think about the kind of stuff he had always thought it best to repress. He very slowly lifted his arms and placed his hands rather stiffly on her slight shoulders. 'Don't thank me, thank Andrew when you see him. I'm only acting for him.'

Buoyant with happiness, Tia took Max down to the refectory, chattering away in answer to his questions, her earlier unease forgotten. 'Do you like dogs?' she asked.

'I've never had one but I believe your grandfather kept dogs when he was a younger man.' And an astute little voice was warning Max not to hand all the bouquets to Andrew when he was supposed to be trying to impress Tia.

Unhappily Max had not a clue how to impress a woman because he had never had to try before and a pair of sparkly diamond earrings was highly unlikely to cut the mustard with Tia. But had he but known it, he had done the one thing calculated to open the gates to Tia's heart and trust.

That Max was willing to arrange for a very ordinary little mongrel to travel to another country simply to please her overwhelmed Tia's every expectation of him and filled her with appreciation and gratitude. He had to be a kind, sensitive man, she decided happily.

Max and Tia were not left alone at the table in the refectory for long. Visitors to the convent rather than the school or orphanage were rare and various nuns arrived to make his acquaintance. Max withstood the onslaught with admirable cool and the inherent courtesy engrained in him by his education. English was in short supply but Max contrived to speak in French, German and Spanish to facilitate the dialogue and Tia was even more impressed. Sister Mariana managed to extract the fact that Max was single and even the explanation that he had not yet married because he had still to meet 'the right woman'.

Once the pleasantries were at an end and Max had regretfully declined an invitation to watch a DVD of the Pope's most recent message in the common room, Tia was spellbound by him, convinced she would never meet a more self-assured and refined, sophisticated male in her lifetime. Not that she had much experience of such men, she was willing to admit. Max smiled at her, dark eyes mesmerising below the thick veil of his lashes, and butterflies danced in her stomach while her heart beat so fast that she felt weirdly dizzy.

Sister Mariana accompanied them back upstairs and showed Max the small seating area on the landing. 'You must have so much to discuss,' she said cheerfully before she headed for her own room.

'Does she think I'm about to jump you or something if you come into my room?' Max asked, shocking Tia.

Paling at the crack, she looked up at him wide-eyed. 'No, she meant to be kind,' she replied stiltedly. 'She knows I would not go into your bedroom.'

As a deep rose flush flowered to chase Tia's pallor, Max recognised his mistake but could not even explain to his own satisfaction why he was so on edge. 'I apologise. I thought the rules were restricting us, which would be a little ridiculous when you are leaving this place tomorrow.'

'It's not "this place",' Tia murmured a shade drily. 'It's been my home.'

'I do understand that but this…all this.' Max shifted a brown hand expressively. 'I'm a complete fish out of water here.'

Tia absorbed the fluid elegance of that physical gesture and marvelled that even his movements could be so graceful. Recognising his discomfiture, she forced a smile. 'Yes. I can understand that. I can only hope I won't feel the same way in my grandfather's home.'

Max gazed down at her, recognising that the laughing, relaxed Tia had gone into retreat as soon as he'd spoken earlier. 'Not while I'm around,' he swore instinctively, feeling ridiculously protective for no reason that he could comprehend.

'Do you live with my grandfather?' Tia asked hopefully.

Having stumbled again, Max almost swore out loud. 'No, but I'm a frequent visitor.'

'I'm glad to hear that,' Tia told him.

Her sincerity mocked all that Max was concealing from her. His strong jaw line clenched. Rain lashed against the window beside them as they stood there.

A sexual tension so strong it almost unnerved him gripped Max, tightening his every muscle into immediate self-disciplined restraint. He connected with translucent cornflower-blue eyes. He lifted his hand and brushed a stray strand of gold hair back from her cheek to tuck it behind a small ear.

That intimate little motion, the brush of his fingers against her ear lobe, seemed to burn a fiery trail across her skin and the breath caught in Tia's throat, the noise of the rain outside suddenly mirroring the tempest inside her. She could feel a tightness in her breasts and a sudden embarrassing surge of warmth between her legs. Still as a statue she stayed where she was, foolishly wanting him to do it again, wanting him to *touch* her. As an adult she wasn't used to being touched except by the younger children. Oh, she had been shown plenty of affection by the nuns while she was still a child but as she'd matured the sisters had naturally become less demonstrative and affectionate and the kind of touching that could remind you that you were not alone in the world was what Tia had missed the most in recent years…only she hadn't realised that until Max broke the ice and showed her that reality.

Max forced his hand to drop back to his side and breathed in slow and deep. He was incredibly aroused and incredibly frustrated but her sheer innocence overpowered and haltered his lust. 'I must phone Andrew. He'll be waiting to hear all about you,' he explained, the Italian accent that had faded over his years in England fracturing every word.

Tia nodded. 'I'll catch Teddy before breakfast so that he can't wander away and lose his big chance to travel,' she joked and, turning on her heel without another word, she left, evidently quite unaware that he had wanted to grab her in the most inappropriate way and kiss her.

Still breathing like a man who had climbed a mountain only to discover another mountain awaiting him at the summit, Max went for a shower to cool off. It was the absolute worst and coldest shower he had ever had but Max, who now took luxury and comfort for granted, genuinely didn't notice, so preoccupied was he with his own thoughts.

## CHAPTER TWO

MORNING DAWNED—but not before Max, who had slept fitfully on his lumpy mattress on a frame that creaked with every slight movement of his body.

He had risen early, craved his usual black coffee and had had to start his day without it. He had immediately contacted his PA to plan for the dog and organise various other bookings.

'Take her to Rio and kit her out,' Andrew had urged effusively on the phone the night before. 'She's a woman. Never met one that didn't like clothes.'

Max's eloquent sensual mouth hardened. He doubted that Andrew would have been quite so chirpy on the subject had he seen for himself how very poorly his grandchild was dressed. Yet her father had visited his daughter and must not have cared. Max marvelled at the hypocrisy of a man who had apparently done much genuine good in the world and yet had utterly neglected his own child. That was at an end though, he reminded himself grimly. Tia's new chapter was only beginning, and a few months down the road she would in all likelihood cringe at what she remembered of her current lifestyle and it would no longer be mentioned because it would become a source of embarrassment to her.

Max was disconcerted at the faint stab of regret he experienced at the prospect of Tia changing radically and losing that innocent openness. She had not learnt guile or the feminine skill to tease and flirt yet.

And that was what had probably knocked him for six the night before, Max judged with a strong sense of relief at that explanation. How did he relate to a woman so different from any he had ever met before? Or slept with? Max's experience lay solely in the field of highly sexualised flirtations that led straight to the bedroom in which there was no before and after to be considered and very little adult conversation.

He had *tried* to tell Andrew that his plan wasn't going to work because Tia was far too 'nice' for him and he didn't have anything in common with nice girls. Virgins were not his style. He had few inhibitions but, coming awake several times during the night, he had acknowledged that seducing a virgin would never feature on any bucket list of his.

Of course, there was a slight chance that she might not be quite that naïve, he reasoned, and then he discarded the suspicion, recalling that moment on the landing when she had looked up at him with a complete lack of any awareness.

Other men would target her and bed her without

a thought, Max acknowledged grimly, anger filling him at the realisation. What the hell was the matter with him? Why was he so conflicted about this situation? He was usually very decisive. *Dio mio!* He could marry her or he could stand back and watch her get her heart stamped on and kicked by some bastard who only wanted her for her inheritance. He could not have it both ways. It would either be him or someone else.

He walked out of the bedroom and was surprised to see Tia seated on the landing with something on her lap. It was the dog. As he moved towards her the dog began to growl. It bared its teeth and would have leapt off her lap into attack had she not restrained the animal.

'Good morning,' Tia said with the most radiant smile that lit up her whole face. 'I've never been able to pet Teddy properly before because I didn't dare smuggle him in here and I fed him secretly…well, not secretly enough it seems.'

Teddy began to bark and she scolded him but Teddy had neither discipline nor manners and he strained forward, snarling at Max as he approached. He had not the slightest doubt that he would be bitten could Teddy have only got free of the piece of twine lead and the makeshift collar he now wore.

'He's not a friendly dog,' Max remarked tactfully.

'He was probably abused. He only trusts me. It's sad,' Tia reflected, still sunny.

'Have you packed?' Max prompted.

'I didn't have much to pack,' she admitted. 'But one of the sisters gave me a bag last night and I used it. I went back downstairs to say my goodbyes then to everyone…'

As her voice thickened and trailed away, tears glistening in her eyes, Max hunkered down at a safe distance from Teddy's snappy jaws. For a tiny dog, he was ridiculously aggressive. 'It's all right to be upset at leaving. As you said, this has been your home for a long time,' he murmured soothingly.

The dark rich tenor of his voice shimmied up and down Tia's spine like a caress and she scolded herself, for she had lain awake more than she had slept the night before. She was attracted to him, of course she was, because he was young and gorgeous and kind. But she had sworn she would not make a fool of herself over him by staring and acting foolishly as she had often seen some of the teenage schoolgirls doing over a handsome young gardener who had worked at the convent for several months. Tia told herself that she was old enough and mature enough to know better.

But meeting Max's glorious black-lashed dark eyes only a couple of feet away convulsed her throat and unleashed the butterflies in her tummy again. She could feel the colour and the heat of a blush building in her cheeks, and as his gaze lowered to her mouth even her lips seemed to tingle with responsiveness. Never had Tia felt so out of her depth as she did at that moment or more aware of her own deficiencies. The teenagers she had once felt superior to had known much more about how to talk and behave with a man than *she* did. When Max got close and she looked at him, she felt almost choked by shyness and awkwardness and every feeling, every sensation she felt was magnified to quite absurd proportions.

For a very experienced man, Max was strangely exhilarated by that blush and he studied her with a weird sense of achievement. She was *not* indifferent, *not* unaware of him. And she was doing what women had done decades before equality transformed the dating scene and waiting for him to make the moves. Flowers, Max thought for the first time in his life in a woman's radius. She would like flowers, being old-fashioned and all that, he decided vaguely.

'We're being picked up in an hour.'

'Mother Sancha has asked us to join her for coffee before we leave but I'll get you breakfast first.'

Max gritted his teeth as Teddy glowered at him over Tia's shoulder and bared his own in a silent snarl of warning. Hate at first sight, Max conceded with sardonic amusement. 'If you could have one special thing, Tia…*anything*, what would it be? There must be things you want—'

'A mobile phone,' Tia told him with a haste that embarrassed her, worried that she sounded greedy.

'You don't have one?' Max queried in disbelief.

'Mother Sancha banned them. She won't allow the girls in the school to have them here. I should explain…' Tia hesitated. 'When I was at school here it was a normal boarding school but that changed as the number of boarders went down. The girls who stay here now are more transient and don't stay for as long. Their parents send them here because they're… troubled,' she selected uncomfortably. 'The sisters have a good record for straightening out troubled teenagers.'

His mouth quirked at that information. 'Yes, I imagine being sent out here to the back end of nowhere and being deprived of even a phone would have a sobering effect on most adolescents.'

'The school fees keep the orphanage going and fund the community work the sisters do!' Tia exclaimed repressively.

'I wasn't mocking the system. I was merely making an observation,' Max challenged.

'You sounded sarcastic,' Tia countered.

'I often am,' Max admitted equably. 'You'll have to get used to nuances like that with people. People don't all think and speak and act the same.'

Tia rounded on him at the foot of the stairs, her ready temper roused at being patronised as if she were still a young girl when she was a grown woman and proud of the fact. 'Do you think I don't know that?' she questioned fierily, an angry tightness marking her small face.

'I think you live in an institution where being different is frowned on and probably have little experience of what life is really like beyond the convent gate.'

'Well, then you'd be wrong because I have often seen the consequences of alcoholism and addiction, domestic abuse and prostitution. There can be few evils that I have not some knowledge of,' Tia argued furiously, hotly dismissing his apparent conviction that she was some naïve little flower. 'Maybe you thought you'd find me on a hill somewhere singing among the wild flowers? Yes, I *am* acquainted with sarcasm, Max!'

Max was taken aback by the display: she had gone from zero to ninety in seconds and lost her temper. 'Does that also mean you need to start shouting at me?' he shot back at her.

Recalled to her wits but still trembling with annoyance, Tia stilled and sucked in a steadying breath, appalled at the rude way she had attacked him. 'I'm sorry. You didn't deserve that rant. I suppose I'm worrying about how I will appear to you and to my grandfather and that I won't suit.'

'You needn't worry about that. If you had horns and a tail, Andrew would welcome you. You're his only relative,' he responded wryly.

'I have a terrible temper. I'm supposed to go for a walk and practise breathing exercises when I get mad, so that I don't lash out at people,' Tia confided guiltily.

'I'm pretty tough, Tia. I can take hard words,' Max countered.

Shame engulfed Tia because this was the person trusted by her grandfather to take her to England, the man who had already ensured Teddy's continuing health. 'I'm sorry,' she said again gruffly.

Max closed a hand on her arm to prevent her from walking away. 'It's OK,' he breathed more forcefully. 'You're right in the middle of a huge upheaval in your life.'

Tia blinked back the tears that had been gathering in hot, prickly discomfort behind her eyes. 'Don't make excuses for me. I was horribly rude.'

'You have fire. I like that, *bella mia*,' Max admitted huskily, his dark deep intonation somehow rousing a curl of heat low in her pelvis. 'I was being patronising and you were right to call me on it.'

'You're very...understanding,' Tia breathed soft and low, locked into his stunning dark eyes as he bent towards her, Teddy's feisty warning growls at her feet ignored by both of them.

And for a split second she actually thought he was going to kiss her and she craved that kiss as she craved water on a hot day, needing somehow to know if that soft, full lower lip of his would be hard or gentle on hers. *Hard,* she decided, lost in a sensual daydream for the first time in her life.

'I have Mr Leonelli's breakfast waiting,' Sister Mariana called down the corridor, and Max jerked back, releasing her wrist, lifting his head again, a telling gleam of feverish colour accentuating his high cheekbones.

*Nearly forgot yourself in a convent,* Max derided for his own benefit, fighting his arousal with all his might while wondering how she would react if she noticed. He was discovering that when Tia looked at him as though he could walk on water, he liked it, and that astonished him.

Tia was in a daze over breakfast. She knew all the facts about sex and had always thought the actual mechanics of the act sounded fairly disgusting: what the man did, what the woman had to allow. But Max had walked into her life the night before and even her outlook on that had changed because she was now putting Max into that couple equation and found that she was madly curious and shockingly excited by the concept. What startled her the most was the deep current of desire rippling through her whenever she looked at him, whenever she even *thought* about him. In his radius her body no longer felt like her own and was certainly no longer fully under her control.

'So, where do we fly from?' she asked as she settled into the four-wheel drive. Teddy was not impressed to be confined in the pet carrier inside it and whined in complaint but his new official owner didn't want him biting Max and she was rather afraid that he might if given even the smallest chance. The little dog she had quietly adored for so long was revealing unexpected traits now that he was being forced to mix with other people.

As for Tia, her eyes still damp from parting from Mother Sancha who featured in her earliest childhood memories, she felt like someone at the start of

‧d all the right boxes. And came with a mas-
eritance, the other side of his brain reminded
ut that wasn't a box he had sought to tick be-
even before he'd accepted Andrew's offer to
nporarily into the CEO job to free Andrew
his unsuccessful treatment, Max had been
ugh in his own right to be satisfied with his
e. At the same time though he relished the
allenge of controlling Grayson Industries.
he acknowledged wryly, was definitely an
siac.

hooped in delight when she saw the massive
ne Redeemer statue, Rio's most striking land-
Max was quick to realise that he was unlikely
e that tourist pilgrimage and he breathed in
ell, at least someone was likely to appreci-
private chapel at Andrew's country house
e older man had had meticulously restored
pe of encouraging his devout son's, Paul's,
England.

n the limousine that had collected them at
ort drew up outside the giant opulent hotel
ey were to stay, Tia was momentarily over-
. '*This* is the hotel? But it's famous.'

A dancing smile slashed Max's beautifully
mouth, his dark as night eyes gleaming. 'I
you would enjoy it.'

lt overwhelmed. That smile engulfed her
al wave, washing away clear thought, ignit-
n all the physical reactions that both thrilled



an adventure and was working hard at concealing that less than cool reality.

'Rio,' Max told her, lifting his darkly handsome head from the tablet he had been using. 'Sorry I'm distracted but I have work email to answer.'

'We're going to Rio? I thought we were going to Belém.'

'We are, but we are flying to Rio before we head for the UK.'

'I love Belém. It's so big and busy,' Tia chattered and told him about the annual boat trip the sisters took along the River Guama to see the Círio of Nazaré procession, which was the biggest and most important religious event in Brazil.

She talked a lot, Max reflected, and culture shock was likely to hit her when she saw the size of Rio de Janeiro because the city of Belém was tiny in comparison. He also wondered what he would do with her in Rio because he had work to do. It was all very well for Andrew to send him halfway across the world for Tia, but Grayson Industries did not run itself and fast decisions had to be made every day to keep Andrew's companies running smoothly. In addition, Max worked very long hours to convince himself and anyone else who cared to quibble that he was fully capable of being CEO of Grayson Industries despite his comparative youth.

'If we're really going to Rio,' Tia said breathlessly, 'I have a school friend there whom I would love to visit. I haven't seen Madalena since we were eighteen and she left school to go home to her family. We write to each other…well, she writes occasionally. She's very busy.'

'Is she one of those *troubled* girls you mentioned?' Max enquired almost lazily.

'Of course not. Madalena was Head Girl in our last year,' Tia told him cheerfully.

'You should spend an evening with her,' Max suggested.

'Yes. It would be wonderful to have the chance to catch up with what she's been doing,' Tia remarked, thinking that she would be listening rather than contributing at any such reunion because Madalena's family was well-off and her former schoolmate seemed to enjoy a dynamic social life. But even so she would very much enjoy seeing the bubbly brunette again. Madalena was a lot of fun and fun was something that had been in very short supply in Tia's life since her school days had ended.

At the airport, they boarded a private jet. Tia was astonished when Max pointed out the Grayson logo on the tail fin and explained that her grandfather owned it. When he had said 'wealthy' it had not occurred to her that he could mean quite *that* level of wealth. She sat quietly in her upholstered leather seat while she was served a delicious lunch. Max pretty much worked and she wondered if that was the norm for him or if rather, and which she felt was very likely, she simply *bored* him. Their lives were very different. They had nothing in common, she



conceded unhappily. What c
businessman of Max Leonelli'
worthy of interest in a girl wh
restricted life in a convent?

Thoroughly depressed by tha
ing herself for the reality, Tia
had quietened down considerab
the carrier. Teddy went to sleep
dozed off too.

As the jet landed at Rio, Ma
isfaction on his morning of wor
recalled his passengers and the
trip to Rio de Janeiro. He was s
the opportunity to get to *know*
women he knew she had not ut
plaint at being ignored. His cons
studied her, her beautiful face
exquisite pillowy mouth more
repose. Teddy's little beady ey
he could sense Max's proxim
and he bared his teeth in a sil

'Get used to me,' Max mu
going away.'

He would marry her. It w
even thought of marriage be
him but Tia was beautiful an
ing. How could any man pos
winning combination in a w
of partners in his bed over t
all the variety that imbued

and unnerved her at one and the same time. She smoothed her fingers down over her best skirt, made of cotton cloth that had once been a pristine white but which now had a creamy tinge. 'I'm not dressed for a place like this, Max,' she pointed out uneasily.

'But you will be soon,' Max told her. 'I've organised a new wardrobe for you. Someone is coming to our suite to measure you and someone else will then arrive with a selection of clothing for you to choose from.'

'Are you joking?' Tia whispered in astonishment.

'No. Your grandfather wants you to have whatever you want.'

'But I didn't ask for clothes.' Tia reddened. 'Well, I know I need them.'

'Let's not make a big deal of it, then. Andrew is a generous man,' Max told her, nodding to the driver to open the passenger door beside her.

Flustered, Tia climbed out, smoothing her skirt again, her palms sweating as she scanned the ornate front entrance and the even more opulent interior she could see through the open doors. Inside she could see elegantly dressed people moving around and her courage almost tanked at that point because she knew how shabby and poor she had to look in comparison. What had passed muster at the convent could not even compare to the smartly uniformed staff surging towards them to pick up their luggage. Teddy was checked in to the equivalent of a luxury kennel and Tia parted with her pet with reluctance.

The dog settled, Max planted a controlling hand to the base of her spine and swept Tia back into the lift, ignoring her resistance. 'Stop acting so nervous,' he breathed in her ear. 'You're a Grayson and your grandfather has made that name something to be proud of. Clothes aren't important.'

It was all right for him, Tia reflected on a surge of brief resentment, for Max exuded the sophisticated, exclusive lustre of a male who had only just stepped off a glossy magazine cover. Every inch of him was groomed and sleek. He reeked of money and self-assurance, neither trait being one she had ever enjoyed, but she knew that Mother Sancha would have agreed with his outlook rather than her own and she gritted her teeth. Within minutes they were ensconced in the lift with their luggage.

The magnificent suite reminded Tia of rooms she had seen on a popular Brazilian soap opera based on a very rich family. The views were stupendous, on one side looking out over the huge city and on the other out over a vast beach and the sea. Every window opened out onto a balcony and the furniture was beautifully upholstered in colours that struck her as wildly impractical for daily use. She followed the porter into a glorious bedroom, walked into an attached bathroom resplendent with marble and mirrors and gold taps. Her fingertips brushed a white fleecy towel and then trailed over the shot silk spread on the bed before withdrawing again.

'Tia,' Max called. 'I have something for you.'

Tia moved forward on uncertain legs, already overcome by her luxurious surroundings and the bewildering suspicion that she had accidentally strayed into someone else's dream. She gazed up at Max, colliding unwarily with his stunning, heavily lashed dark as night eyes. Her breath feathered in her throat and her heart slammed with sudden force against her breastbone as he extended his hand. 'For you from me,' he intoned. 'It's all charged up and ready to use.'

It was a mobile phone with a sparkly cover, the sort of cover a teenager might have admired but Tia was not fussy. With a whoop of pleasure at finally receiving what she had long wanted, Tia whirled breathlessly round the room. Madalena had kept on sending her phone number as if Tia could somehow magically conjure a phone out of thin air but she had kept her friend's letters. 'Thank you, Max,' she said.

Max was a little disconcerted not to receive another hug, had indeed braced himself for one, but Tia, did he but know it, knew she had to be more circumspect around him once she had understood how much he attracted her. She didn't want to behave like an infatuated schoolgirl and make a fool of herself.

The flowers were the next delivery, a gorgeous display of white lilies and foliage arranged by a maid in a crystal vase. 'For…*me*?' Tia whispered breathlessly, a fingertip stroking a velvety petal in appreciation.

'Of course for you…'

Tia could not imagine why Max was giving her flowers when they were already in each other's company and he had nothing to thank her for. The romantic angle, she discarded entirely as an explanation, having decided during the flight that allowing foolish fancies to take over her brain was likely only to lead to her humiliation.

Max got the message that he was not making his interest obvious enough and that was when he regretted not paying more attention to her while they were airborne. He studied her glowing face as she caressed the lily and imagined that small work-roughened hand gliding over a far more responsive part of his body and anticipation leapt through him like a sudden flame ready to burst out of control. The stirring of enthusiasm at his groin was unmistakeable and made him ache. He didn't know why she had that instantaneous effect on him. Indeed, his lack of control around Tia annoyed him because he hadn't suffered from the affliction of involuntary arousal since he was at school.

'You like the flowers?'

'Yes,' she whispered distractedly. 'I love flowers. I always dreamt of having a real garden of my own.'

'I thought you wanted to be a teacher,' Max remarked, because the Reverend Mother had shared that with him.

'I was willing to be one to get the training and the education. In my life it's always been a question of *not* what you want but what is possible,' Tia explained. 'There's a teacher training college in Belém and I thought that studying there would be achievable but my father wasn't willing to pay for it and that was that.'

'Andrew's country house has beautiful gardens,' Max told her, watching the tip of her tongue steal out to moisten her full lower lip as she looked up at him and almost groaning with the force of his arousal.

His dark eyes were gleaming like gold ingots and Tia couldn't drag her gaze from his lean, darkly beautiful face. Without even knowing what she was doing she took an infinitesimal step closer and Max reached for her almost simultaneously, hands sliding round her back and yanking her into contact with his lean, powerful body with a sexual insistence and impatience that should have shocked her but which instead thrilled her.

It was Tia's first kiss—first *everything*, really—and the hard, hungry pressure of his beautiful masculine mouth crashing down on hers unleashed so many sensations in her body that she felt dizzy. The tips of her breasts tingled and stiffened, pushing against the coarse cotton material of her top. A sliding warmth prickled between her thighs and made her press them together tightly. Suddenly she was insanely conscious of a part of her body she never thought about, of the sensitivity and the shocking level of physical awareness she had never known before.

His tongue licked along the fullness of her lower

lip and then nibbled at the tender swollen flesh before his tongue plunged into her mouth and withdrew. At that point her legs would have folded under her had he not literally been holding her upright with his hands because the sexual vibrations assailing her only intensified. A choked gasp was dragged from her as he spread his fingers across her narrow shoulder and held her there to kiss her breathless.

Max was fiercely fighting an insane urge to carry her into his bedroom when the knocking at the door finally penetrated the fog of his passion. What the hell was he doing? he asked himself furiously as he jerked back from her, almost overwhelmed by the passionate response he had won from her. He wanted more, he wanted *so* much more that it took a lot longer than the few seconds he had to get a grip on himself before he opened the door.

Four women greeted him with wide smiles and swiftly identified themselves as the team engaged to provide Tia with a new wardrobe. Shooting her a cloaked glance to note that she was very flushed and dazed in appearance, he urged her to take them into her bedroom.

*Diavolo,* he castigated himself as soon as the bedroom door closed. He had jumped the gun, offered too much too soon and probably shocked her, but going slowly with a woman, much like talking in a normal way, was something Max had never done before. And he had utilised all the finesse of a bull in a china shop, an awareness that infuriated him as he stomped off to change and have a cold shower to chill the fever still burning through him. It was not as though he were sex-starved, he reasoned angrily with himself, so why that lack of control? That mad grab and hold making-out session, which was not his style at all?

Relieved to escape the immediate aftermath of that embrace with Max, Tia was happy to be distracted by measurements and catalogues depicting various styles. She had only wanted jeans and tee shirts and some decent shoes but there was, she discovered in amazement, a vast area of choice from which to make selections. The little girl and disappointed teenager who had never got to have pretty clothes triumphed in the adult she had become and she went a little crazy before panicking and surging back into the other room to find Max.

'What's my budget…? I mean, how much can I spend?' she pressed anxiously.

'There is no budget. Order anything that takes your fancy…handbags, shoes, *everything*,' Max stressed. 'You'll need it all in England and it's better to arrive prepared.'

Tia surveyed his darkly handsome features with wondering appreciation. Had ever a young woman been so blessed as she was at that moment? she marvelled, smiling widely at him. She could buy anything she liked and Max, the man of her dreams, had kissed her, which meant that he was attracted to her as well, even if she suspected that he hadn't quite intended to kiss her when he had.

Was Max struggling with the same feelings she was struggling with? Feeling buoyant at that suspicion and walking on air in the belief that the growing strength of her feelings was being reciprocated, Tia vanished back into the bedroom.

## CHAPTER THREE

'I DON'T WANT TO,' Tia said simply as Afonso, one of Madalena's male friends, tried to pull her into the bedroom that had just been vacated by another couple.

'Thought you wanted to lose that V-card…' In the face of her refusal, Afonso managed to both smile and sneer simultaneously. He was good-looking and he knew it, his lack of familiarity with rejection obvious to her.

'Maddie was joking, for goodness' sake,' Tia declared, wishing that that were true of her former best friend but no longer quite sure because she felt as if she was learning the hard way that four years could change a friend into someone she barely recognised.

'No, she wasn't,' Afonso insisted, still unwilling to accept that no meant no in Tia's case as he pulled her against him with a possessive and determined hand.

He was drenched in cologne and she could hardly breathe that close to him. She gave him a dispassionate glance, hating the swimming sensation in her head from the alcohol she had already told Madalena she didn't want to drink. Not because she was stuffy and prim, as Maddie had insisted she was. She had refused more alcohol as soon as she'd felt her body overreacting to that second large drink. No, indeed: the very last thing Tia wanted to risk was getting drunk at a wild party full of strangers, none of whom she felt she could rely on.

It was ironic that she wasn't having anything like the fun she had once assumed such social events delivered when she was younger. Fun, she rather thought now, depended on the company you were in and she knew she was in the *wrong* company. Losing her virginity with some stranger on a night out had no appeal for her. Maddie, however, had decided it was a terrific idea, pointing out that the first time was always 'rubbish' for a woman. Tia had said nothing because that conversation had taken place in a group setting and she had been embarrassed at having her sexual ignorance talked about in public as if it were solely a subject for amusement.

Nothing with Maddie had gone as Tia had planned and hoped. When she had phoned Maddie that afternoon, the brunette had invited her over that very evening and Tia had naively pictured a chatty session of catching up. When she'd arrived, though, Maddie had already been entertaining a bunch of friends and the first thing she had done was insist that Tia borrow some of her party clothes to go out with them.

Stripped of her jeans and tee, Tia had found herself being crammed into tight satin shorts and a backless top, both garments exposing far more of her body than she was comfortable with. But the other women had been wearing similar outfits and she had wanted so desperately to try to fit in and not be the party pooper Maddie had suggested she was that she had kept her reservations to herself.

Maddie was engaged to a handsome young businessman. Unhappily the couple had vanished within minutes of arriving at the party, lumbering Tia with Afonso and his sidekicks, whose only topic of conversation appeared to be dirty, rather infantile jokes. Before Maddie had finally abandoned her, however, Tia had seen a scattering of powder below her school friend's nose and had suspected that she was using drugs, which probably explained her unfamiliar highly extroverted and bad-tempered behaviour.

'So where exactly are we here?' Tia asked again.

'Why do you keep on asking me that? I don't know the address. It belongs to Domingos Paredes. We're in Jardim Botânico. It's an exclusive residential area.' Afonso trailed a suggestive hand down her bare back, making her shudder. 'Play your cards right and you could end up swanning around a house like this. I bet there's nothing you want more than to be a wife and a mother. Some guys go for that. Come on…stop being such a prude.'

'I'm not a prude,' Tia argued as Afonso backed her up against the wall. 'I don't feel that way about you.'

'But you haven't even given me a try,' Afonso protested, hands roving all over her and trying to go in for a kiss but stymied by the manner in which Tia hastily jerked her head away.

'Let go of me!' she told him with sudden loud, angry emphasis. 'I don't have to put up with this if I don't want to!'

Afonso backed away a step and swore viciously at her. 'You're a freak,' he told her nastily. 'Nothing but a damned freak!'

As the young Brazilian stalked back into the crowded main room of the party in a rage of wounded vanity, Tia was trembling and tears were burning the backs of her eyes, making them throb. She walked towards the back of the big house, stepping over prone bodies and entwined couples to escape the worst of the noise. On the terrace she dug out her new mobile phone with a shaking hand and rang Max, who had programmed his number in.

'I want to come back to the hotel,' she told him chokily.

'What's the address?' Max queried. 'Has something happened?'

'I'm at a party and someone called me a freak. It's probably the truth,' she told him in a shaky rush. 'I don't know the address but I know who the house belongs to and the area. I can't get a taxi because I have no money.'

'I'll find out where you are and pick you up as soon as I can.'

'I'll wait outside.'

'No, stay indoors where it's safe,' Max instructed. 'And calm down.'

Ashamed of the tears blurring her vision and what felt like her general uselessness as the strong independent woman she was determined to be, Tia approached a female in the bathroom queue and finally asked for the address, which she duly passed on to Max.

'Where the hell have you been?' Maddie demanded of her in the hall. 'And what did you do to poor Afonso? When I last saw him, he was really into you.'

'I wasn't into him.'

'Well, it doesn't matter. We're all moving on now to this great club.'

'I'm going back to the hotel, but thanks for bringing me out,' Tia said very politely.

'Mother Sancha did a real number on you, didn't she? You really don't know how to enjoy yourself at all,' Maddie declared pityingly. 'If I'm honest I always thought you'd join the flock.'

'I never had a vocation,' Tia admitted, wondering how long it would take for Max to arrive and sitting down on a chair by the wall because she was lightheaded. 'But I'll admit that I don't know how to enjoy myself the way you do. I'll return these clothes back to you tomorrow.'

'Oh, don't be silly. I won't wear them again after *you've* worn them,' Maddie confessed with a little moue of distaste at the idea. 'I'd only be dumping them.'

Tia reddened and nodded, more uncomfortable than ever. In the convent, they had utilised and recycled everything possible. 'I'll collect my jeans,' she said stubbornly. 'They're my very first pair.'

'And that says it all really, doesn't it?' Maddie said almost sadly as she walked on by.

Her colour fluctuating, Tia thought about Max and admitted that what she had felt in his arms had also told her all she needed to know. After all, once he had kissed her she had immediately known that she didn't want anyone else kissing her. But what if on *his* terms it had merely been a casual kiss? Of the same sort that Afonso had offered? How did she tell the difference? How did she *know*?

All that she knew was that Max's mouth on hers had been the most glorious and exhilarating feeling she had ever experienced and she literally couldn't wait for him to do it again. But would he *want* to do it again? And how did a woman encourage a man to make that kind of advance without being brazen about it? She was mortified to acknowledge that she would have gone into a bedroom with Max without a word of protest. What did that mean about her? That the convent teaching of purity before marriage had hit stony ground when it came to her? Or that while she was aware of that moral ideal, it was *only* an ideal and she was equally well aware that many people experimented with sex before marriage?

Max was in the back of a limousine speeding through the Jardim Botânico area and he felt like the biggest bastard in the world. He was supposed to be taking care of Tia but he had no experience of looking after anyone and, clearly, he'd fallen at the first hurdle. Instead of accompanying her to her friend's house, he had let her go alone and he had not even ensured that she had money with her. Admittedly he had first established that Madalena Perez was the daughter of a respected diplomat and seemed a safe companion. Although it hadn't occurred to him that Tia could be going out on the social scene, it should have done and he *should* have been there. *Shoulda, coulda, woulda*, a minatory voice sneered in his hind brain. He had ducked his responsibility because he'd wanted to work.

What did that say about him?

After all, Tia was infinitely more precious to Andrew Grayson than his empire and Max knew it. As Max's future bride, she should be equally precious to Max and deserving of special attention, but he had let her down. He had organised a spa grooming appointment for her the next day, not to mention a trip to see the giant religious statue on top of Corcovado Mountain, but those were superficial treats and would be of little consolation to her when she was as hurt and upset as she had sounded on the phone.

Max helped himself to a second drink, his inbuilt alcohol monitor screaming reproach at him for the choice. As the son of a violent alcoholic, Max usually only had one drink at a time, never more, fearful that he could have inherited a gene that could make him more likely to fall into his father's addiction. Not that there was anything good to be said for *any* of the genes Max had inherited, he conceded with grim self-loathing. Not for the first time, he reminded himself that his mother's sister, Carina, his aunt, had been a perfectly normal woman in decent employment and respected by all who knew her, but it didn't remove the sting of shame that any recollection of his own seedy beginnings invariably unleashed.

Even in the surge of arrivals and departures that saw cars constantly moving up and down the driveway to the big villa, Tia was primed to recognise the one that contained Max and she had bounced up off her chair even before he appeared at the door, head and shoulders wider and taller than the two younger men who arrived there before him. When someone dragged open the door and her expectant gaze landed on his darkly beautiful features she felt ridiculously tearful and had to restrain herself from throwing herself at him like a child.

Max, for his part, was frankly shocked rigid by the vision of Tia in skin-tight red satin shorts, a silky, glittery, barely there top and Perspex stripper heels. He had relished the shape of her in the jeans she had worn earlier that afternoon, almost painfully aware of her long slender legs and her delicate but highly feminine curves at hip and chest. But braless and in shorts, *everything* was on view and he had an outrageous urge to yank his jacket off and drape it round her because the blatant sexuality of what she brandished in such an outfit was a very poor frame for the young woman she actually was.

'Max…' she breathed, hurrying towards him, her eagerness to leave the party unconcealed in the huge cornflower-blue eyes pinned to him.

Max herded her outside towards the limo, striving honourably to ignore the little bounce of her small firm breasts as she went down the steps and the flash of long creamy inner thigh that led up to her scarlet-defined crotch. But he was still a man and he got painfully hard just picturing that first full-frontal view of her again, his brain quick to conjure up the definition of thin satin over a woman's most intimate area. And then the rage took a hold of him like a rejuvenating bolt of lightning that burned out all sexual response, which in the strangest sense was a relief for him.

As soon as the driver closed the passenger door on them, Max rounded on Tia, dark eyes flaming gold with instinctive fury. 'You don't *ever* go out dressed like that again!' he thundered across the car at her.

Taken aback by that sudden attack, Tia bridled and her eyes flared a darker blue in angry confusion. 'What on earth are you talking about?'

'You look like a pole dancer or a stripper. You're showing too much skin. Where did you get those clothes? I can't believe the stylist authorised those shorts.'

'What's a pole dancer?' Tia enquired icily, her spine very stiff in her corner of the car because who did *he* think he was to tell *her* what he thought she should be wearing? He was a man and what she wore was none of his business.

'Not the sort of woman you want to be mistaken for.'

'Madalena loaned me these clothes and I wasn't comfortable in them,' Tia admitted grudgingly. 'But her friends were wearing the same sort of thing. And the stylist didn't *authorise* me to choose clothes today, I made my *own* choices and they were probably pretty boring choices because I didn't pick any party stuff like this.'

'People…men in particular will judge you by what you wear,' Max bit out with a raw edge, his anger compressed but still burning like a solar flare inside his chest because every time he thought of the men who had enjoyed the same view of Tia that he had had, he got furious all over again.

'That's very old-fashioned,' Tia replied without hesitation. 'Anyway Maddie made sure our companions knew I wasn't as sexy as I looked because she told them all that I was a virgin,' she confessed boldly, far less embarrassed by that reality than she had been earlier that evening after Maddie had forced her to deal with that topic in public.

'She *told* them?' His nostrils flared with distaste,

an ebony brow flying up in frowning query. 'What the hell was she playing at?'

'She tried to persuade me to lose my "V-card", as she called it, by going into a bedroom with one of the men,' Tia confided. 'I refused and that's why I got called a freak.'

'She's *not* a friend,' Max pronounced, helplessly cast back to his own experience of betrayal by a friend he had trusted when he had been a teenager. 'Definitely not a friend. Friends don't try to harm or humiliate you.'

Tia winced. 'Think I've kind of worked that out for myself, Max. I even suspect that dressing me up like this was part of the joke for her. She wasn't the girl I remembered from school.'

Max closed a hand over hers where her small fingers were curling defensively against the leather upholstery. 'Not your fault. It was mine. I shouldn't have let you go alone. I didn't even make sure you were carrying money.'

'No, Max…' Tia yanked her hand from beneath the comforting warmth of his although it took effort to voluntarily break that contact. 'Don't treat me like a child you have to take care of. I have to learn how to handle myself and not depend on others. I'll find my way. I won't be a freak for ever.'

'You're *not* a freak,' Max growled, forcibly closing his hand over hers, all the more tense because he knew he had utilised that same word in his head when he'd first learned about her unusual background. 'You're only a little out of step with the modern world and given time that will quickly fade. Your father should've been shot for leaving you at the convent even after you finished school.'

'He didn't want to be bothered with me and out of sight was out of mind for him. My mother wasn't much different,' Tia sighed. 'I think they were both a bit shallow and selfish when it came to personal relationships. With Dad, all his passion went into his missionary zeal and he didn't really have room for anything that interfered with that. My mother, I think, is more driven by money and social position.'

His brows had drawn together. 'You've *met* your mother? I assumed you hadn't seen her since she left your father when you were a baby.'

Tia compressed her generous mouth and looked steadily back at him, for the first time striking him as being more mature than her age on paper. 'Curiosity brought her to the convent. She visited me when I was thirteen to explain why she'd left me behind.'

*'Che diavolo...!'* Max exclaimed in surprise. 'That must've been some explanation that long after the event.'

'No, it was quite simple.' Tia's luscious soft mouth compressed. 'She broke up with the man she originally left my father for and then she met another man, a rich man, and they married. Although her second husband knew she had been married before, he didn't know she had left a baby behind her. They went on to have children together, two boys and another girl, I seem to remember.'

'Your half-brothers and half-sister,' Max commented.

Tia shrugged a slight shoulder in dismissal of that familial label. 'But they don't know I exist and my mother doesn't want them to know because she's afraid she would lose her husband and her wonderful life here in Rio after keeping me a secret for so long. *He* was more important to her than I could ever be. It was really that simple.'

For some reason that non-judgemental tone of acceptance made a kind of murderous rage swell up inside Max's broad chest. His own parents had been appalling in terms of family affection and Tia had not done that much better, yet her parents had not even had the excuse of ignorance, poverty or addiction. He breathed in deep in the silence and swallowed hard, for there was really nothing he could say to her that she hadn't already worked out for herself. She was shrewder than he had given her credit for, convent-bred or not. He was both disconcerted by that acknowledgement and relieved, for the more intelligent and wary she was, the quicker she would adapt to life as Andrew's heiress. And as his *wife*?

Max stiffened, squaring his wide shoulders, his handsome mouth flattening. He refused to even think about that aspect this early in the day. If he did marry Tia as Andrew had urged him to do, no actual wedding would take place for months. Max refused to rush into anything. Max liked structure, order, strategic planning. He didn't do impulse or invite disruption in any field and would never have scaled the heights he had without serious self-discipline. With Andrew expecting to survive another six months at least, Max planned to utilise a good part of that time to move in unthreatening, measured steps with Tia while she got to know her grandfather.

The limo drew up outside the brightly lit hotel. Max sprang out first and then disconcerted her by peeling off his suit jacket and draping it round her shoulders as she emerged from the car.

'Is that really necessary?' Tia enquired, reeling a little and struggling to find her balance in the ridiculous heels as the fresh air engulfed her.

'*Sì*...if you can turn *me* on this hard and fast when I'm striving to stay cool, I imagine other men will stare too, and I am assuming you would prefer not to be stared at and lusted after,' Max murmured in a raw undertone, astonishing her with that abrupt and unexpected admission. 'On the other hand, if you enjoy being the centre of male attention, give me my jacket back...it's entirely your decision.'

*She* turned him on. Tia was exhilarated by that grated confession and clutched protectively at his jacket, which fell past her knees, revelling in the intimacy of the silk lining still warm from his skin and the faint evocative fragrance of his cologne that still clung to the fabric. She breathed that fragrance in like an addict. Unlike Afonso, Max didn't drench himself in scent. The attraction *was* mutual. Of course, she had suspected that after the kiss but Max had been very businesslike and detached when they had been alone after the stylists had departed and she had felt discouraged. Now standing in the lift, wrapped in Max's jacket, struggling not to study him with lustful eyes lest he instantly recognise her shamelessness, Tia felt transformed, shedding the sense of failure and mortification that events at the party had wakened in her.

If Max wanted her too, *could* anything else matter to her? In that instant nothing mattered to Tia but the way she was feeling. For so long she had been locked away from all the normal experiences she should have begun enjoying in her teen years. That was when she should've enjoyed her first kiss, falling in and out of love, dating, gossiping, learning all the many things that a young woman had to learn as she grew up. But Tia had been denied that adult education and now that she had met Max, she was greedy to catch up with everything she had missed out on.

Butterflies were whipping up a storm in her tummy and her heart was beating very fast. Max glanced down at her and swiftly looked away again, his strong jaw line pulling tight to define his superb bone structure even more cleanly.

'You'll want to go to bed now. You have an early start in the morning,' he informed her briskly as he opened the door of their suite and stood back for her to precede him, the courtesy making her feel delightfully feminine.

'I'm not a child, Max,' Tia reminded him afresh.

Max gritted his teeth together, for he had not been impervious to the way she had studied him in the lift. But that kind of early intimacy wasn't on his schedule and he refused to deviate from what his logic told him was the right and proper way to embark on any sort of relationship with Tia Grayson. That one kiss had been dynamite and he didn't play with dynamite and he didn't lust uncontrollably after virgins like the creepy little loser who had already tried to lure her into bed that night, he reasoned.

'I'm twenty-two in three months' time,' she reminded him, wriggling her slight shoulders to remove his jacket and settle it on the arm of his chair.

Her golden mane tumbled round her lush little face and that was when he finally nailed her startling resemblance to a poster of a film star his mother had much cherished as a feminine ideal. It was those wide perfect cheekbones, those bright cornflower-blue eyes, that delicate little nose and that wickedly sultry mouth. He was transfixed as she settled down on top of his jacket, long graceful legs stretched out. She angled her head back, the elegant pale line of her throat revealed, and as her spine arched her firm little breasts thrust out below the fine material of the draped top and Max's rigid controlling schedule went out of his mind so fast she might as well have flipped a switch.

…andfather expects me to look after you,'
…ed her tautly, uneasily conscious of the
…e at his groin while idly wondering
…d disgust or intrigue her before hast-
…he thought as unwise.
a… …g a terrific job,' Tia told him sun-
…e de…
…'s rules… …at undeserved accolade. 'Not

…hat Max … denied, leaping upright to
…oral pur- … nforce her conviction. 'You
calmed me down and came to pick me up. I feel safe with you—'

Max expelled his breath in a pent-up hiss. 'But you're *not* safe with me. I'm not qualified to be playing a big brother role around a gorgeous woman—'

Tia stood her ground, a slight giggle at his terminology escaping the ripe pink parted lips that were his sole focus while she wondered if he really meant that flattering word he had ascribed to her. 'I don't want you as a big brother, Max, and I'm glad you can be so honest because *I* want to be honest too…' she began.

Max made a last-ditch effort to save her from him and from herself and disconcerted her by suddenly bending down to scoop her up into his arms and stride at speed towards her bedroom, where he intended to stow her safely out of reach. He burned for her but it wasn't that simple. He would not allow himself to be tempted beyond the boundaries he had

set. He didn't want her to be honest with hi
he couldn't *be* honest with her. Andrew had
den Max to even tell his granddaughter tha
terminally ill because he wanted to handle
formation personally. Andrew wanted Tia ke
dark about everything: his business empire
inheritance, his fears, his fiercely protecti
for her to marry Max. Regrettably, Andrew
simply made Max's role more difficult.

For a heady split second, Tia assumed t
was taking her into her bedroom for imm
poses and in the mood she was in she was fully on board with that idea, but when he laid her down on the wide bed he started to straighten and pull back. It occurred to her then that he was actually physically putting her to bed like a misbehaving child and, outraged by that suspicion, she shot out a hand to grab his sleeve and pull him back to her.

'Max!' she censured sharply.

Max jerked back another step and hit his head, a crushing blow on the ornate wooden strut of the four-poster bed frame. For an instant he literally saw stars and swayed and, seeing that, Tia succumbed to guilt and regret.

Scrambling up on her knees, she grabbed his hand worriedly. 'That was my fault. Are you all right? That was quite a thump you got.'

*'Sì...'* Max conceded, blinking rapidly in an effort to clear his fuzzy head and dismiss the pain while slowly turning to look down at her. Her blue eyes

were so honest and anxious and the luscious mouth below them so perfectly plump and inviting that the ache at his groin almost made him groan out loud.

'Sit down for a minute. You've gone very pale,' Tia told him.

'I don't need to sit down.' A shred of sanity remained in Max's bemused brain and in it the bed loomed large as a trap of catastrophic proportions.

'Sit down, for goodness' sake.' Wondering if he had concussion because he seemed dazed, Tia used her hand on his to yank him down on the mattress beside her. Rising to her knees, she reached up to feather her fingers gently through his tousled black hair to feel the faint swelling beneath. 'We should go to the hospital.'

'It's only a bump, Tia,' Max groaned, turning his head to look at her in wonderment because after the childhood he had endured bumps and bruises, including broken bones, were nothing new to him.

'If I hadn't been…messing around…' Tia selected her wording with care, her conscience still twanging as she marvelled at her own misplaced and mistimed boldness '…it wouldn't have happened.'

And what was about to happen wouldn't happen either, Max continued inwardly, absolutely enthralled by the upturned pink swell of her tantalising mouth and discovering too late that that was the true trap, not the bed, after all, because he leant down as if being drawn by invisible strings to touch his mouth to hers.

And holy hell, she tasted like sweet juicy strawberries and the hot, spicy night air. Max fisted a hank of golden hair in one hand and he crushed her soft pillowy lips beneath his own with fervour, hunger leaping through him with unstoppable force.

His tongue flicked against the sensitive roof of her mouth and delved deep and a massive ripple of seductive sensation slivered right through to Tia. Unlike Max earlier she had no doubts about what she was doing or what she was inviting. Max was, basically, the man of her dreams and when Tia wanted anything she threw her heart and her soul into getting it with a stubborn, steady-minded resolve that her grandfather would have recognised as his own. Max was kissing her again, which meant he wanted her as much as she wanted him. Of course, he had tried to put the breakers on this exact development, she acknowledged absently, loving that he hadn't wanted to rush her into anything too soon, recognising what she saw as being an honourable streak in his character.

But Tia made her mind up fast and she was eager to live the life she had been denied for so long, in fact, grab it with two greedy hands and run as fast as she could with it…

## CHAPTER FOUR

TIA SUCKED IN a great lungful of air as Max temporarily released her mouth. There was a golden glow of what she fully recognised as lust in his stunning eyes. It didn't have to be love, she told herself, she wasn't looking for love yet, was content with a dose of healthy normal lust. In the future, there would be plenty of time and opportunity for her to fall in love. But even so, nothing had ever felt so necessary as Max's sensual mouth plundering hers and the sweet, sliding invasion of his tongue.

Her body was all pulled taut and needy with responses that were new to her. Her breasts felt ridiculously sensitive, the tightly beaded tips pushing against the scratchy fabric of her top.

'You should make me wait for this,' Max growled soft and low, conflict in his hungry gaze as he perused her.

Already flushed, Tia's face burned at that unsought advice. 'I can't believe you're saying that to me. I thought you wanted me.'

'Doubt there's a man in Rio who wouldn't want you, *bella mia*,' Max assured her helplessly. 'But I also don't want you to have any regrets.'

'Why on earth would I regret this?' Tia questioned, sitting lithely up to reclaim his drugging mouth again for herself, hands settling on his warm, wide shoulders, fingers flirting with the silky tips of his black hair. The buzz in her body wouldn't let her stay still or act compliant.

Max loosed the halter tie at the nape of her neck and found the soft pouting swell of her breasts with his hands, catching her nipples between thumb and finger to pluck at the swollen buds, pushing her back against the banked-up pillows as she writhed.

The liquid heat at the heart of her went into a frenzy when he touched her breasts. She pressed her thighs together, head rolling back and shifting restively against the pillow as he released her reddened lips to close his to her straining nipples. The light was burning and her lashes flickered on a sudden view of Max's dark head over her bare breasts. For an instant she went rigid, mortification threatening to claim her because she wasn't accustomed to being even partially naked in front of anyone and the shock of that glimpse was extreme. *Are you a woman or a mouse?* a little voice asked at the back of her head, and the words bubbling on her tongue died there. She knew what she was doing, she *did*, she told herself, trembling as the heat between her thighs mounted with every tug of his mouth. How could anything that felt so good be wrong?

Max rearranged her petite body on the bed the better to enjoy her. Her nipples were a delicate tea-rose pink, darkened by his attentions, and her breasts exquisitely shaped but bare handfuls to a man used to better-endowed women. Even so, Max was enthralled by her porcelain-pale skin and the satiny softness of it, even while he was deciding that while Teddy the dog might be a little on the porky side his owner was a little too thin and needed feeding up. He wrenched at the shorts and the thin material ripped, startling her, troubled blue eyes opening to belatedly recognise that he was still fully clothed.

'Take your shirt off,' she whispered.

Charmed by that instruction, Max dealt her a slanting grin. 'You wouldn't think you were a first timer at this.'

Forcing herself to keep her hands loose on the bedspread when self-consciousness prompted her to cover her breasts from his view, Tia watched him strip off his shirt.

'I'm a quick learner,' she told him, her mouth watering as he exposed the coiled lines of muscle across his abdomen and flat stomach. The dampness at her core increased and she couldn't drag her gaze from his lean, powerful body. His bronzed skin sheathed rippling muscles, a broad chest and narrow hips stretching down into long, hair-roughened thighs and around there her scrutiny bounced hurriedly upward again, noting the trail of dark hair that ran from his navel to disappear below the band of his boxers and, the whole time, striving not to think nervously about his obvious arousal.

Was she stupid? She was annoyed with herself for that schoolgirlish embarrassment. He was aroused, of course he was, just as she was. She wasn't about to let the horror stories told by Maddie and her potty-mouthed friends of their first sexual experiences to unnerve her...*was she*? She was a grown woman, not an adolescent playing with forces she didn't understand.

Max came down on the bed, kneeling over her, caging her with his big body and a rush of excitement snaked through her, every nerve ending jangling with anticipation. He had done this before, hadn't he? Of course he had, she told herself instantly. But it didn't always pay to make assumptions about people, she conceded.

'You've done this before...haven't you?' Tia pressed awkwardly.

And Max, who didn't embarrass easily, in fact who would have said he was impervious to embarrassment, could feel his face heating up. 'Yes,' he pronounced flatly, reasoning that, as she had waited, it was not impossible that he could have been the sort of rare male who waited too for that one special experience. And unfortunately, that set off a whole train of conjecture in his head about what Tia might want from a man. An innocence that matched her own? A guy who went to mass? A perfect shining angel of a male, who was honest and decent and religious? He didn't think he was any of those things.

'A lot?' Tia could not resist prompting uneasily. 'I mean…er, have you had a lot of women in your life?'

Wide, sensual lips compressing, Max simply jerked his head in acknowledgement, wishing that the heat in his face would subside.

Her own face warming, Tia closed her eyes but still saw the troubled dark gold of his gleaming eyes below the black fringe of his lashes. She had embarrassed him and she shouldn't have done that. At least he had been honest, though; at least he hadn't lied about it, she reflected ruefully.

'I think this would be a lot more challenging if we were both virgins,' Max breathed curtly while thinking he had never thought to share such a conversation in his life with a woman. Then again, he hadn't bargained on a Constancia Grayson figuring in his future, had he? And Tia was very much one of a kind.

'You're probably right,' Tia conceded.

'But you're also probably disappointed,' Max breathed and gritted his teeth, suddenly feeling furiously out of his depth, wondering where he was planning to go with the dialogue and finally registering just how off his game he was that he didn't actually know.

'No. I don't think I am,' Tia murmured, huge blue eyes opening to dreamily survey him, pale fingers smoothing from his shoulder down over his chest in a considering caress that blanked his mind and locked his tongue, because the one thing Max did know at that precise moment was that he wanted her hands *all* over him.

Max lowered his dark head, drawn by forces he didn't even understand. She might want some ideal, perfect male but guess what? She was getting *him* and she could learn to deal, he thought, with the kind of raw aggression that powered him through the business world. He focused on that soft, pouty mouth and went back hungrily for more, smiling into the kiss as her spine arched and her whole body reached up to him, responding to *his* expertise, wanting *him*.

Long brown fingers smoothed along her thigh and when she emerged from that kiss he was working his sensual path down over her squirming length and at some stage of the proceedings her knickers had gone and she felt shockingly, wickedly naked. But before she could even process that discovery, Max parted her thighs and began to do something she had read about but had never dreamt she would actually experience.

The wave of heat and mortification that pulsed through her shaken body was intense. In an abrupt move, she reached down and snarled her fingers into the black luxuriance of his hair and then he licked her, *there*, where she had never dreamt she would be so intimately touched, and such a pulse of shattering excitement gripped her that she fell back helpless against the pillows.

He did it again and she gasped, neck lifting, breasts straining, suddenly in the hold of something seemingly much stronger than she was. Her body writhed of its own volition, a crazy pressure building at her aching core, and her nails dug into his shoulders. He was ravishing her, *tormenting* her with pleasure, she thought wildly, in thrall to pure sensation. She trembled, shook, emitted muffled cries, utterly out of control, her entire being locked to the feeling of his fingers entering her previously unbreached body. His tongue flicked across the tiny bundle of nerves he had exposed and it was as though her body detonated, the pressure peaking and the aftershocks passing outward, sending a coiling energy blast of delight to pull at her. Sated, dazed, she fell back against the pillows in wonderment at what sex was all about.

'No, you do not get to go to sleep now, *bella mia*,' Max warned her thickly, sliding up her relaxed body to gaze down at her with molten golden eyes awash with hunger and need.

And Tia realised for possibly the first time that it wasn't all about her and guilty colour washed her face, a new tenderness sliding in its wake as she noticed the tension etching his lean, darkly handsome features. As he lifted her legs and tilted her up to him, she only just restrained herself from wrapping her arms round him and hugging him for giving her a superlative introduction to the physical that bore no resemblance to the sexual horror stories she had been subjected to earlier that evening.

'I hope this doesn't hurt much but it might,' Max breathed in a driven undertone. 'I haven't been with a virgin before.'

'That's all right,' Tia framed in a rush, stretching up her head and claiming a kiss from that wide, sensual mouth that had taught her the meaning of pleasure.

As Max kissed her back, doing that flick of the tongue thing again that enthralled her and reanimated the heat in her pelvis, she felt him push against her tender flesh, inch by inch pushing for entry into her untested body. She was insanely conscious of his every tiny movement, equally aware that he had prepared her as well as he could. And it seemed to work until he drove deeper and there was a sharp pinch of pain that forced an involuntary gasp from between her parted lips. And he stopped.

'No...go on,' Tia urged, gritting her teeth, her body even more primed than she was for the great reveal, indeed the churning liquid heat in her pelvis craving exactly that development.

Max thrust home, crazily aware of her lush inner walls clenching round him. *'So good,'* he ground out helplessly, revelling in every tight, hot, wet atom of her welcome and somewhere around then he lost himself as he had never lost himself in a woman before.

Hands clenched on her hips, he pulled back and then plunged into her again, hard and fast. The shock of it thrilled through her tender body like a storm warning. It was the most extraordinary pleasure she had ever experienced. As he pounded into her, her hands clawed in his hair and then into his shoulders and then down his back, the excitement and the pressure rising and rising until she could no longer contain it. Her heart thundering in her ears, her head jerking back and forth on the pillows, she felt that mighty surge of sensation gripping her womb and throwing her high as outer space again. She thrashed beneath him, unable to contain the ecstasy as convulsions quaked through her satiated body.

In the aftermath she felt so heavy, so languorous, she was bemused. 'That was…don't have the words…'

In bed or out of bed, Max rarely had words with women, preferring to escape intimacy with silence on the sensible grounds that what wasn't said couldn't be misinterpreted. But Tia had both arms and both legs wrapped around him and he was trapped. 'That was the best sex I've ever had,' he mumbled thickly, his head now aching so badly he couldn't think straight.

In consternation at that awareness, Max reeled out of bed, as dizzy and disorientated as a drunk, and he finally appreciated that there was something badly amiss with him, something worse even than his usual punishing migraines. 'Sorry, feeling weird,' he framed with difficulty. 'Think I must be overtired…'

Tia leapt out of bed as he sank down on the rug. 'You need a doctor,' she gasped.

'Don't want a doctor,' Max told her predictably.

Fortunately, Tia discovered that a doctor was easily obtained by the helpful hotel staff. The minutes that followed her call were frantic. Between fetching Max a glass of water and finding and getting some clothes on her naked body before registering that Max was naturally equally naked, she felt harassed and anxious and very guilty. It was concussion, she knew it was, having seen the effects before in the convent infirmary. Max rambled on about his susceptibility to migraines and the medication he wanted her to get from his room but Tia only grabbed clothes from the built-in units in his room.

Persuading him to get back into the bed was a challenge but he didn't appear to own pyjamas or a dressing gown and the only item of clothing she managed to get him into was a pair of boxers. By that stage the doctor was at the door and she had to answer it flustered and barefoot, but such was her apprehension for Max that she wasn't concerned.

The young, chatty doctor wanted Max to have a hospital scan but Max was as immovable on that score as concrete laced with steel. For some reason, he didn't like hospitals and he didn't like scans. After considerable pressure from the worried doctor, who was equally convinced that Max had concussion from the blue-black bruising and the swelling that was visible when his hair was parted, Max agreed to attend the hospital the following morning. Discussing the treatment Max required, Tia saw the doctor out of the suite.

'Tia…' Max called almost as soon as she was out of his sight.

Breathless, Tia sped back and studied him, wondering what was normal for Max because the doctor had asked her that question when telling her to look out for abnormal behaviour. But how much did she know about the man she had just slept with? Next to nothing, came the answer. Ashamed of that reality, Tia reddened.

'I can't simply lie here in bed like I'm ill!' Max bit out in frustration.

'You have to. You're very dizzy and if you fall I couldn't get you up on my own,' Tia pointed out sen-
[illegible] practical nature taking charge. 'It's mid-
[illegible] considered the [illegible] hours.'
[illegible] gement that she [illegible] your grandfa-
[illegible] ore of a shock. [illegible] nd little sleep,'
[illegible] flatly, having [illegible] from below the
[illegible] reality. 'We're [illegible] y contriving not
to flinch. There she was [illegible] ful downfall, the film-star beauty ruffled but no less appealing, golden hair tumbled round her heart-shaped face, blue eyes sparkling. She had a sort of effervescent glow about her. Knowing that he was about to douse that glow didn't improve his mood.

'Tia… I didn't use protection,' he divulged in a harsh undertone of self-blame.

'What do you mean?' she prompted uncertainly.

Max groaned out loud, for that naïve question said it all as far as he was concerned. He had taken cruel advantage of her innocence, he conceded grimly. 'I assume that thump on the head left me disorientated. I didn't use contraception with you.'

Belated comprehension striking her, Tia froze and her complexion turned pale and clammy. 'Oh,' she framed in dismay.

'As I'm regularly tested there is no risk of disease,' Max assured her, his intonation brusque. 'Believe it or not, I have never before had sex without using protection. Obviously one doesn't want consequences…'

'Consequences…you mean, me getting pregnant,' Tia gathered, her brain still struggling to handle the deeply unwelcome surprise he had dealt her.

How could she have been so fooli[illegible] so carried away that she hadn't even [illegible] risk of pregnancy and the acknowledg[illegible] could *be* that irresponsible was even m[illegible]

'Clearly that's a risk,' Max spelt ou[illegible] watched her pale and flinch from that [illegible] both young and healthy. There could definitely be consequences.'

Only that morning, Tia had wakened in the convent, still naïve and ignorant about matters that other young women took for granted at her age. Now all of a sudden it felt as though she was being subjected to a frightening crash course on what adulthood demanded and she was appalled by her carelessness.

attend the hospital the following morning. Discussing the treatment Max required, Tia saw the doctor out of the suite.

'Tia…' Max called almost as soon as she was out of his sight.

Breathless, Tia sped back and studied him, wondering what was normal for Max because the doctor had asked her that question when telling her to look out for abnormal behaviour. But how much did she know about the man she had just slept with? Next to nothing, came the answer. Ashamed of that reality, Tia reddened.

'I can't simply lie here in bed like I'm ill!' Max bit out in frustration.

'You have to. You're very dizzy and if you fall I couldn't get you up on my own,' Tia pointed out sensibly, her practical nature taking charge. 'It's midnight anyway and it's only for a few hours.'

'I don't go to bed at midnight like your grandfather. In fact I'm used to late hours and little sleep,' Max murmured drily, studying her from below the lush black fringe of his lashes, barely contriving not to flinch. There she was: his beautiful downfall, the film-star beauty ruffled but no less appealing, golden hair tumbled round her heart-shaped face, blue eyes sparkling. She had a sort of effervescent glow about her. Knowing that he was about to douse that glow didn't improve his mood.

'Tia… I didn't use protection,' he divulged in a harsh undertone of self-blame.

'What do you mean?' she prompted uncertainly.

Max groaned out loud, for that naïve question said it all as far as he was concerned. He had taken cruel advantage of her innocence, he conceded grimly. 'I assume that thump on the head left me disorientated. I didn't use contraception with you.'

Belated comprehension striking her, Tia froze and her complexion turned pale and clammy. 'Oh,' she framed in dismay.

'As I'm regularly tested there is no risk of disease,' Max assured her, his intonation brusque. 'Believe it or not, I have never before had sex without using protection. Obviously one doesn't want consequences...'

'Consequences...you mean, me getting pregnant,' Tia gathered, her brain still struggling to handle the deeply unwelcome surprise he had dealt her.

How could she have been so foolish? She had got so carried away that she hadn't even considered the risk of pregnancy and the acknowledgement that she could *be* that irresponsible was even more of a shock.

'Clearly that's a risk,' Max spelt out flatly, having watched her pale and flinch from that reality. 'We're both young and healthy. There could definitely be consequences.'

Only that morning, Tia had wakened in the convent, still naïve and ignorant about matters that other young women took for granted at her age. Now all of a sudden it felt as though she was being subjected to a frightening crash course on what adulthood demanded and she was appalled by her carelessness.

She had forgotten all common sense, everything she had been taught about how to look after herself and stay safe. She couldn't even recall how many years it was since she had been assured that purity was the only certain way to avoid an unplanned pregnancy. So informed, her classmates had giggled and exchanged superior glances while whispering remarks about modern birth control. But, Tia told herself unhappily, her hindsight and regret came a little too late to the table to be helpful. It was done; wrongly or rightly, it was done.

'We'll have to get married,' Max informed her without hesitation. 'Immediately. In this situation where I was entrusted with your care, it's the only possible remedy. Your grandfather trusts me. If there's the smallest chance that you could be pregnant I need to marry you now.'

In silent disbelief, Tia stared back at him. Perspiration beaded her brow. That was the moment that Tia registered that, not only did she not want to be pregnant, but she also didn't want to be married either. No, not even if Max resembled a Renaissance prince and took her to heavenly heights in bed. What Tia had dreamt of for so many years, what she had always craved was…*freedom* and independence. And nobody needed to warn her that there was little wriggle room for freedom in either matrimony or motherhood.

# CHAPTER FIVE

BENEATH MAX'S INTENT, measuring gaze, Tia had lost all her natural colour and her bright eyes veiled as she studied the highly polished wooden floor instead of him. He realised instantly that Tia was not receptive to the idea of marrying him and it was a shocking wake-up call for a man who had spent years on the social scene being relentlessly pursued by ambitious young women in search of a rich husband. Tia had slept with him but she didn't want to *marry* him.

It was a revelation and it hit Max's ego hard because, he realised angrily, he had placed too much importance on her obvious attraction to him. Very possibly right now she did not feel much different than he did after a one-night stand. She might have enjoyed herself but that didn't mean she was eager for a repeat.

'You have a very expressive face,' Max murmured grimly.

'That's why I'm *trying* not to look at you!' Tia protested with emphasis. 'Mother Sancha always knew what I was thinking almost before I did. It's just… what you said about getting married startled me. I wasn't expecting that.'

'As I see it, we don't have much of a choice,' Max intoned, his delivery bordering on curt in tone. 'Bringing you home to Andrew unmarried and pregnant would be a disaster, possibly more for *me* than you I'll admit. I fully believe that your grandfather would forgive you for anything but he has higher expectations of me…and I'm not a member of his family.'

The gruff note on which he completed that very honest little speech unexpectedly touched Tia's heart. For possibly the first time she appreciated that, while he might not be a relative, Max was undeniably fond of Andrew Grayson.

'I have no idea how you even know my grandfather or what your relationship with him is,' Tia reminded him uncomfortably. 'Do you work for him? Are you a neighbour? A friend?'

Max breathed in deep, already inwardly monitoring what he was willing to tell her and all the many things that he planned to take to the grave with him. 'I was born in a small Italian village. My background is poor and rather sleazy,' he admitted starkly. 'When, for reasons I won't go into, my parents were no longer able to look after me, my mother's sister, Carina, who worked in England for Andrew, agreed to give me a home. She became my guardian when I was twelve. Your grandfather generously paid for my education. I lived under his roof during the holidays, not as a guest, though, but as the housekeeper's nephew in the housekeeper's apartment.'

Tia was taken aback by all that he revealed, having assumed that Max came from much the same sort of privileged and financially comfortable background as her father. Her lashes fluttered rapidly as she absorbed that new information, for it *did* put a different complexion on their situation. Clearly, Max felt he owed Andrew Grayson a debt for his kindness and did not feel that he could afford to rely on the older man to forgive or overlook any mistakes he made. Did Max think that getting entangled with Tia counted as a mistake? Suddenly, she was very much afraid that that was exactly how he viewed their passionate encounter.

'Everything that I am today I owe to Andrew's generosity,' Max confessed harshly. 'I don't want to do anything that distresses him. He's eighty and he's…' unusually he hesitated '…frail.'

'Our getting married could distress him,' Tia suggested.

'No. Don't forget that Andrew is from an earlier generation of men. He still sees marriage as the best source of happiness and security for a woman,' Max told her flatly.

'So, you're willing to marry me simply on the off chance that I could conceive,' Tia recapped. 'I understand that but I would prefer a husband who wanted to marry me for a more conventional reason like love.'

'I won't lie to you,' Max murmured in a tone of frustration. 'I can't offer you love. I was only in love once in my life when I was very young and I hated the effect it had on me. But I *can* promise to be caring and supportive…and, assuming it's a normal marriage, faithful.'

Inwardly reeling from that declaration, Tia plonked herself down in a corner armchair and gazed back at him. Her body still ached from his possession and that spur of recollection sent a snaking coil of heat down into her pelvis when she studied his lean, strong face. She respected his honesty even if she didn't like his embargo on love because she strongly suspected that, given sufficient time, she could fall for Maximiliano Leonelli like a ton of bricks. After all, he was offering her almost everything that she would eventually want…only she hadn't wanted to find it quite so soon after leaving the convent.

She should have thought of that reality before she'd shared her body with him, she reflected guiltily, should have thought of who he was and who she was and how her grandfather might react to that intimate connection. But she hadn't thought one sensible thought since Max had exploded into her safe little world, she conceded. He was lean and dark and beautiful and his sophistication and charisma had stolen her wits. She suspected that from the outset she had been behaving rather like an infatuated teenager, all overexcited and encouraging, wildly impulsive while never counting the cost. Or even considering the question of repercussions. What if she *were* to conceive a child?

Wasn't that the real bottom line? Wasn't she being horribly short-sighted and selfish when she thought regretfully of the freedom she had planned to embrace in England? The putative career choices and socialising she had dreamily envisaged? In their own way, weren't such aspirations rather similar to the single-minded selfishness that had persuaded her own parents to abandon her? A dependent baby hadn't fitted in with either her father or her mother's plans. Once their marriage had broken down, Tia had become an unwelcome inconvenience to Paul and Inez Grayson. Was she to take the same attitude to her own baby, were there to be one?

Everything strong and ethical in Tia cried out against that attitude. If there was to be a baby, that baby's needs should be placed central and first, not sacrificed to her self-interest. She would behave better than her parents had, she told herself urgently. She could make sacrifices if necessary and rearrange her own priorities if she became a mother. But naturally all of that would be easier to do if she had the father of her child by her side to help. Whether she liked to admit it or not, Max's proposal *could* be a lifeline and one that she would very much need if she had a baby.

'Can't we wait and see if we have anything to worry about first?' Tia asked, her colour high.

'I don't think we should risk your new life in England starting out under a cloud,' Max admitted truthfully. 'Your grandfather would be upset if we had to suddenly confess all and get married in a hurry. We could get married here in Rio and return to England as a couple. It would be easier.'

'But it could also be quite unnecessary. I may not be pregnant,' Tia pointed out uncomfortably.

'And if that proves to be the case, we can reconsider our situation at a later date, free of all other concerns,' Max stated with an almost imperceptible wince, thick lashes dropping down on his eyes to shield them from the strong light, his chiselled jaw line clenching at even the prospect of her conceiving.

Scolding herself for her preoccupation, Tia rose to switch off the lamps, so that the only light entering the bedroom was shared from the reception room next door in a wide triangle that plunged the bed and Max into semi-darkness.

'Thanks,' he sighed.

Tia drew in a decisive breath. 'I'll marry you if you honestly believe that that's the best option we have. I don't want to do anything to upset my grandfather either. After all, without his intervention, I would still be at the convent.'

Relieved by her assent, Max relaxed his wide naked shoulders and rested back on the pillows. 'Use my room and go to bed now. It's ridiculous that the doctor told you to sit here and keep me awake all night. Believe me, without my migraine medication I'm in too much discomfort to fall asleep.'

'I'm not leaving you alone,' Tia answered stiffly. 'If I'm going to be your wife, it's my duty to look after you.'

'Don't kill me with enthusiasm,' Max quipped, cringing behind that humour at the label of 'wife' but far more unnerved by the prospect of a pregnancy.

After all, Max had never planned to have a child. *Ever.* He didn't want to pass on what he saw as his murky genes. He didn't want to face the challenge of being a father when his own had been such a monster. All he had ever wanted was a reasonably peaceful, solitary and successful life. But between them Andrew and Tia had tripped him up, thrusting a giant spoke into his structured and controlled existence, throwing up worries and vulnerabilities he had never had to face before. He didn't want to brood about that misfortune though. Life was always challenging, he reminded himself impatiently. And most men would not consider a very beautiful, very sexy wife a burden…

Why did *he* have to be different? But he knew the answer, didn't he? Born of violence, he didn't want to take the risk of forming a permanent relationship with a woman or having a child of his own because he could never quite trust himself, could he?

As his ever vigilant and distrustful aunt had often reminded him, 'Who knows what you'll be like when you grow up? I can only do my best with you but blood can tell in the next generation, and I'm sure you don't need me to tell you that your father was a brute and your mother was delusional.' It had been one of Carina's favourite speeches and it had ensured that Max never once forgot his sordid start in life.

Unaware of her future husband's bleak thoughts and falling far short of her duty of care as a potential wife, Tia dozed off, exhausted by the day she had had. When she wakened it was late into the morning and she was no longer in the chair, she was lying on the bed with a cover thrown over her, and Max was nowhere to be seen. Assuming he had returned to his own room, she went for a shower, revelling in the refreshing beat of the water against her skin, so very different from the weak lukewarm trickle that had purported to be a shower at the convent. Reluctant to put on her crumpled clothing again, she made use of the fleecy robe on the back of the door and emerged, stilling when she saw Max, fully dressed and apparently restored to normality, in the bedroom doorway.

'Can you get dressed quickly? I've ordered breakfast for you but we're running late for your appointment.'

'I have an appointment? Where?' Tia walked barefoot over the polished floor, fighting to keep her voice level and her expressive face still because her mouth had run dry and her heart was pounding. Clothed in a light grey suit that exuded the exclusive expense of personal tailoring, Max, from the smooth olive planes of his exquisite bone structure to the deep-set drama of his black-fringed golden eyes, was simply breathtaking.

'One of those women's grooming places,' Max proffered. 'I had my PA organise it for you yesterday because I thought you would enjoy the experience. They'll do your nails and stuff like that.'

Tia nodded, a jolt of happy anticipation bringing a sudden smile to her tense mouth. At the party the night before in the company of much better groomed women she had been mortifyingly conscious of her unstyled hair, the ugly callouses on her hands and her short nails. Although she had been raised to believe that vanity was a sin, when she had still been at school with Maddie she had experimented with make-up just like every other girl there. Once Maddie had moved on with her life beyond school, however, Tia had had nobody to share those little vanities with.

'I will enjoy it. Have you been out?'

'I went for the hospital scan first thing,' Max admitted, surprising her. 'I have concussion, which will heal on its own. I feel fine.'

Tia wanted to slap him for not waking her and allowing her to accompany him. Concussion and he just shook the injury off as though it were nothing? Wasn't that taking macho male denial of weakness too far?

'I'm relieved that you got checked out but surprised because you seemed so against it last night.'

'I don't like hospitals but I'm not stupid. I've had concussion before and it was more serious on that occasion.' Max shrugged a dismissive shoulder while watching her pull various garments to consider from the wardrobe. 'Wear the blue dress. It'll highlight your eyes,' he advised, striding back into the other room.

Clad in the blue dress, Tia slid her feet into light sandals. She rubbed her pale cheeks to lend her wan reflection a little colour. She looked tired, not her best and she marvelled at Max's undeniable energy after his accident the night before. He'd had concussion *before*? Had he got into a fight with someone or been involved in a car accident? Frustratingly there was so much she didn't know about Max Leonelli and she wanted to know more.

An astonishing array of dishes greeted her in the room next door. Teddy had been released from his kennel for an hour and he was standing guard below the table, growling every time Max moved, but when he saw Tia he raced to greet her in a tail-wagging, doggy-licking surge of happiness.

Wryly watching the delighted reunion taking place a few feet from him, Max waved an eloquent hand over the food. 'I didn't know what you liked so I ordered a selection.'

'But this is so wasteful,' Tia whispered instinctively. 'I won't eat half of this.'

'This is your life now,' Max countered with level

assurance. 'You have the luxury of choices. You don't have to make do any more.'

With a guilty sigh, Tia lifted a plate and served herself. 'It'll take a lot of getting used to.'

'It does,' he agreed. 'It was like that for me when I first arrived in England. But you'll soon adapt. We're getting married in forty-eight hours.'

Tia almost dropped the plate, cornflower-blue eyes huge. 'How is that even possible?'

'You can thank your Mother Sancha for organising it for us. Fortunately you hold dual citizenship, which simplifies matters, but the Reverend Mother certainly knows how to get things done quickly and sidestep any awkward rules,' Max declared with visible appreciation. 'Father Francisco will conduct the ceremony in the convent chapel and the ceremony will be screened live on social media for Andrew's benefit.'

Tia stared back at him wide-eyed, the *pão de queijo* baked cheese roll in her hand forgotten. 'My goodness, how have you arranged all that this early in the day?'

'It's almost noon. My work days usually kick off at dawn,' Max told her gently.

*I'm getting married,* Tia thought dizzily. Married to Max. But only because she might be pregnant, she reminded herself darkly and her face heated as that visceral surge low in her belly made her mortifyingly aware of the dulled ache that still lingered between her legs. Nothing to be proud of there, she reflected tightly, bitterly aware that she had grabbed at her first chance of freedom without properly weighing up the advantages and the disadvantages. And yet when she looked at Max across the table, her mind was blank of disadvantages and she was more conscious of the swollen sensitivity of her nipples and the audible hitch in her breathing. She seemed to be as susceptible to Max as Teddy was to all forms of food.

Tia thoroughly enjoyed her trip to the beauty salon. She had never had her hair professionally trimmed or styled before and could barely credit that her very thick hair could be subdued into a flourishing silky mass that tumbled quite naturally round her face. Her hands were softened and her nails transformed into pearly pink elegance. Every inch of her was moisturised and polished and shaped and after a light lunch she sat entranced while she was expertly made up, watching every move the cosmetic artist made because she wanted to be able to copy the look for herself. For the very first time ever she revelled in being a woman.

Max went rigid the minute he saw her walk out to the limousine. Without the smallest enhancement, Tia was naturally beautiful, but fresh from a professional salon she became eye-catching enough to stop the traffic. Rich swathes of honey-blonde hair bounced round her narrow shoulders, framing that wide cheekboned, heart-shaped face to perfection.

'You look incredible, *bella mia*,' he murmured, dark deep-set eyes raking over her flushed face. 'I had planned to take you on the tourist trail this afternoon but I'm afraid you have a more pressing need to pick your wedding dress. A selection is being brought to the hotel.'

Tia blinked. 'I was wondering what I'd wear.'

'All the trappings. Your grandfather will expect it.'

But *nothing* was happening as Tia had once expected it and events were moving far too fast for her to handle with calm. Inside herself she was a massive heap of nerves and insecurities and doubts. She was marrying the first man she had ever slept with, marrying practically the first attractive man she had ever met, to move to a new country and meet a wealthy grandfather, who was a stranger but to whom she owed her opportunity to make a new life. But it wouldn't be the new life of freedom that she had once naively envisaged; it would be a different life built round a husband and even—potentially—a child. How could she possibly be a good or effective mother when she barely knew how to survive in the modern world?

# CHAPTER SIX

SISTER MARIANA CRIED when she saw Tia in her wedding dress, insisting, however, that her tears were happy tears. The older woman had explained that now that Tia was getting married the nuns believed they could feel secure about Tia's future and stop worrying about her welfare. Max, it seemed, now occupied a starring role as Tia's protector in the dangerous new life she was embarking on.

Tia was misty-eyed too as she absorbed her reflection in the glorious confection of lace and tulle that shaped her figure and fell to her feet. She was willing to admit that it was a gorgeous dress even if it was far from being her dream dress. The demands of a convent wedding had made the more fashionable gowns she had been offered inappropriate and Tia had settled for traditional and modest, ruefully aware that that combination would best meet fond hopes. Having to please other people rather than herself had become so much a part of Tia's character that it had come naturally to look away from the short flirty dress she would have preferred and choose the one that swept the floor instead. It wouldn't always be like that for her, she told herself soothingly. Somewhere in her future there would be a time and a place when she could put herself first and stop worrying about pleasing other people…wouldn't there be?

It was an anxious inner question and Tia had struggled with it many times over the past forty-eight hours. Max had made no attempt to be intimate with her again and his restraint had only heightened her insecurity. How much did Max genuinely want her? How did he *really* feel about her? Was he truthfully only marrying her because there was a chance that she could conceive? In short had her body been her only real attraction? And if he could so easily resist her now, what would their marriage be like? Lukewarm? Practical? Unhappily for Tia, she was hot-blooded and passionate and she needed and wanted more.

The day before she had met her grandfather for the first time during a video call. His warm interest in her had been reassuring but his gaunt features and the fact that he was seated in a wheelchair had driven home the reality that Andrew Grayson was every bit as frail as Max had implied. That reality had saddened Tia, making her wonder for how long she would have the great gift of an actual caring relative in her life. Although Andrew had urged Max to take her away on a honeymoon before bringing her home to England, Tia had agreed with Max that they should return as soon as possible.

Tia saw Max waiting for her in the chapel, very tall and dark in his formal suit beside the small, rotund figure of Father Francisco. His likeness to a Renaissance prince in a medieval painting was intense, from the high smooth planes of his stunning cheekbones to the fullness of his sensual mouth. Beneath the black fringe of his spiky lashes, the dark aggressive glitter of his eyes entrapped her and the butterflies in her tummy broke loose again. But in their wake came a deeper, more visceral reaction that was anything but innocent, a tight clenching at the heart of her that she recognised as sexual desire, and her cheeks burned as if she was wearing that need on her face for all to see.

Max watched Tia walk down the short aisle towards him. Her slender figure enhanced by fragile lace and floaty layers, she looked as delicate and beautiful as a spun-glass ornament. One glimpse of that exquisite face and that captivating smile and her grandfather had been totally enchanted. Max's reaction was infinitely more physical, his muscles tightening as he tensed, scorchingly aware of his arousal. He had had to fight himself to stay out of her bed before the wedding but he had won that battle. Max needed to be in control of every aspect of his life; anything less struck him as weakness and he refused to be weak, particularly with a woman. He had made that mistake once in his life and paid dearly for it; he would not make the same mistake again.

'You're a lucky devil, Max,' Andrew had pronounced feelingly on the phone after his first glimpse of Tia. 'She must get her looks from that Brazilian mother of hers, certainly not from my side of the family tree. We were all homely and plain. When you saw her you must have felt like a lottery winner.'

*Not so as you would notice,* Max affixed wryly to that assurance. He was about to be married at the age of twenty-eight when he had once assumed he would be a single man all his days. In some ways, he was still in shock from the fallout of that sudden life change. But the rush marriage and the possibility of consequences were entirely his own fault, he conceded grimly. Blindsided by his bride's extraordinary beauty, he had succumbed to temptation and he had lost control like an overexcited teenager. Why was he worrying? How did he even know he *could* father a child? Maybe he shot blanks, he thought hopefully, and his anxiety at the prospect of fatherhood might yet prove to be a waste of energy.

As for being a married man, he thought as they knelt, a bride that looked like an earthbound angel had to be a huge encouragement for any male wary of settling down. Tia gripped his fingers as though she were in fear of drowning when he eased the gold ring into place. She needn't have worried. A lot of change was coming her way but Max would look after her in every way and to the very best of his ability. He hadn't needed a wedding ring to accept that responsibility though; he would have cared for her simply out of respect for Andrew Grayson. And sliding his own ring on when Tia struggled to get it over his knuckle, he smiled with satisfaction, knowing that as Tia's husband he was also becoming a member of Andrew's family and finally a recognised part of someone's cherished family circle. In all his life Andrew had been the only person willing to overlook Max's frightful background and have faith in him as an individual in his own right.

Boarding the Grayson private jet at Belém, Tia fingered the delicate gold crucifix Mother Sancha had given her and breathed in deep. She was a married woman but she didn't feel the slightest bit married when her bridegroom had yet to even kiss her. As he took his seat, Tia glanced at Max from below her lashes, more and more convinced that he was no longer as attracted to her as he had once been. Why else would he be so distant?

'I'd like to change into something more comfortable,' Tia confided soon after take-off.

Max showed her into the sleeping compartment. She wanted to slap him for his air of courteous detachment. It was their wedding night, after all. Tia had a quick shower and, smothering a yawn that had crept up on her out of nowhere, she donned the filmy turquoise shorts and thin top she had chosen for the occasion. The *occasion*, she mocked herself, her soft mouth down-curving. Was she supposed to go out there and throw herself at him when he was probably working? March down the aisle stripping as she went? Laughter shook her slight frame and another yawn pulled at her lips. She lay back against the pillows, just for a moment to relax and regain her energy, and that was the last thing she knew.

Max swore under his breath when he found his bride fast asleep: a siren in turquoise silk, deliciously pert nipples visible through the fabric, long, pale, slender legs bare. His earthy visions of orgasmic sex were grounded. He wanted to fall on her like a starving man at a banquet because he was so hard he ached, but it had been a very long day and her rapturous reception in England would last even longer. In any case, he *needed* to learn control around Tia, Max reminded himself resolutely, still slightly unnerved by the way in which she had broken through his defences from the outset.

Sheathed in a hot-pink dress, jacket and perilously high heels, Tia joined Max for breakfast. 'Where did you sleep last night?' she asked him bluntly.

'Right here. The seat reclines. I didn't want to disturb you,' Max responded smoothly.

'A normal bridegroom would have shaken me awake,' Tia murmured only half under her breath.

His dark golden eyes flared in surprise. 'I beg your pardon?'

'So you should,' Tia told him roundly, refusing

to back down. 'It was our wedding night and we spent it apart.'

'Perhaps I was trying to be considerate.'

'The next time you get the urge to be considerate, run it by me first,' Tia advised waspishly.

Sardonic amusement flashed across Max's lean, strong face. 'I'm not the most democratic guy you'll meet. I tend to take unilateral decisions.'

Tia frowned. 'That won't work for me. I believe that marriage should be an equal partnership.'

'Duly noted, *bella mia*,' Max drawled, more amused by that fiery note in her nature than persuaded to change either his outlook, in which marriage would make very little difference to his life, or his strategy in how best to integrate a wife into his daily schedule.

Teddy was parcelled off to a quarantine kennel to fulfil UK pet regulations. He would stay there for a few months until he had passed a final rabies test. Misty-eyed at that enforced parting, Tia clambered awkwardly into the limousine that collected them from the airport, displaying a long, slender stretch of creamy thigh.

'You have fabulous legs,' Max heard himself say, his attention riveted to that shapely expanse of pearly skin.

Tia smiled at him, honey-blonde hair falling across her cheek, because his phone had been ringing since they landed and he was finally ignoring it and paying heed to her instead. She had every respect for a man with a strong work ethic but not when it came between her and what she wanted. And what she wanted was a man who acted like a new husband. Circumstances might have dictated that they shelve any prospect of a honeymoon, but that didn't mean it was all right for Max to behave as though they had been married for twenty years. She stretched out her legs, encouraging the hem of her dress to shimmy higher up over her thighs. It was hugely important for her to feel wanted by Max because nobody had ever really wanted or needed her before.

'Are you trying to tempt me?' Max intoned thickly.

Tia rested innocent blue eyes on him. 'Why would I try to do that?'

And Max forgot his ringing phone and his strategy and how considerate he ought to be and simply grabbed her, tugging her across the car and down onto his lap. Long brown fingers darted below the hem to stroke up a satin-smooth inner thigh and rake across the taut stretch of her knickers, skimming her most tender flesh with his nails.

Thoroughly disconcerted, Tia gasped into the mouth that plunged hungrily down on hers. It was as if fireworks were detonating inside her. Her whole being was locked into the provocative exploration of his fingers. She was hot and damp and tender and she had never craved touch the way she did at that moment, her body pushing up into his hand, her thighs splayed, her nipples hard little buds that tingled.

'As you see, I don't need that much encouragement,' Max growled into her ear as he yanked at the garment preventing him from reaching his objective. He traced the heart of her, finding her as aroused as he was. He eased his finger in while his thumb brushed back and forth across her most sensitive spot and before she knew where she was or what she was doing, Tia yelped and bucked. Her excitement peaked so fast she was electrified and she arched and sobbed with intoxicated pleasure as the thunderous waves of release crashed through her entire body.

'And neither, it seems, do you,' Max declared, treating her to a wickedly appreciative appraisal that shot even more colour into her flustered face.

Tia was stunned by what had just happened between them. Within minutes excitement had sent her body racing from zero to sixty. With a trembling hand she retrieved her underwear but dug it into her bag, intensely aware that while she was satisfied, *he* was not. She slid closer, small fingers smoothing uncertainly over a lean, muscular thigh, awesomely conscious of what was concealed below his trousers.

Max caught her hand in his. 'Not here,' he breathed in a roughened undertone, a little taken aback by her readiness to experiment but very much excited by the unexpected promise of that adventurous vibe. 'Later, *bella mia.* I shouldn't have touched you here in the car. We need more privacy.'

A giant blush of self-reproach engulfed Tia in what felt like a head-to-toe flood. She didn't have the sexual confidence to argue with him but she didn't like the fact that he had contrived to do what he wanted but was now denying her the same freedom. She felt controlled and that annoyed her. Perhaps she would have done it wrong, she told herself in consolation; perhaps she would have humiliated herself had she continued. Or perhaps her boldness had turned Max off. She stole a glance at him and discovered, with a faint little smile of feminine satisfaction tilting her full mouth, that that was not the problem.

Tia spoke little until the limo turned off the road down a long driveway edged by mature woodland.

'Redbridge Hall, your grandfather's country house. He grew up here,' Max explained. 'His father bought the place before the First World War. Andrew has a town house in London as well but he rarely uses it. I live in a city apartment.'

Tia stared as a rambling Tudor mansion surrounded by lush trees appeared in front of them. The patterned red-brick walls were matched by tall arched and mullioned windows that reflected the sunlight. 'My goodness,' she whispered. 'It's huge.'

'I believe there are twelve bedrooms,' Max remarked.

'There are a lot of cars here,' Tia noted, because at least ten luxury vehicles were parked on the gravelled frontage. 'Are there people staying?'

'I doubt it. It looks more as though Andrew has given way to his need to show you off.' Max bit back a frustrated exclamation because he had advised the older man to allow Tia a little time to adapt to her new surroundings before plunging her into a social whirl.

'Who on earth would he want to show me off to?'

'Friends and family.'

*'Family?'* she queried with greater interest.

'Although you're Andrew's only blood relative, his late wife, your grandmother, had several siblings, so you do have a bunch of cousins on that side of the family,' Max told her, his lean, darkly handsome features stiffening because most of her cousins resented his very existence, not to mention his business connections with and his closeness to Andrew.

'Cousins. That should be interesting,' Tia commented, stepping out with care in her high heels, already missing Teddy's reassuring presence.

Her grandfather awaited her in a big crowded drawing room. Andrew Grayson beamed and opened both his arms. 'Come here, my dear, and let me have a closer look at you,' he urged.

While she sat beside the old man, the guests drifted over to meet her. 'I'm Ronnie...' A pretty brunette with adorable twin girl toddlers clinging to her legs gave Tia a harassed but very friendly smile.

There were too many names and faces for Tia to absorb all at once. She got mixed up about which were siblings and which were couples, but she was overwhelmed to finally have relatives eager to make her acquaintance. Throughout the session, Max stayed anchored nearby and Andrew frequently consulted him. Tia noticed that most of the visitors were daunted by Max and that in company he seemed much more aloof and remote than he was with her in private. But she was grateful for Max's support when she was faced with more searching questions about her years in Brazil, her mother and her father's activities, for he parried the more challenging queries with an unblemished cool that she could never have matched.

'So, you only married Max yesterday?' Ronnie shook her head in wonder as she poured tea for Tia, her warm brown eyes brimming with curiosity. 'A whirlwind romance, I gather, and I must admit that *that* was a shock. Max always strikes one as a very controlled, cold-blooded businessman, not the type to do anything madly impulsive, but then the rule book goes out the window when a beautiful woman is involved. And you are, if you don't mind me saying so, remarkably beautiful and probably very photogenic. The press will go mad for pictures of you when they find out you exist.'

Unable to relate to the concept of Max being in any way cold-blooded, Tia had gone pink. 'Why would the press be interested in me?'

'Are you serious?' Ronnie rolled amused eyes in emphasis. 'Andrew's long-lost granddaughter from Brazil gets married to the CEO of Grayson Industries? Andrew is a very rich and important man and

Max is renowned in the business world and on the social scene.'

'I haven't grown up with that background the way you have,' Tia said uncomfortably.

'Oh, neither did I. I grew up on a farm. Your grandmother may have married a tycoon but the rest of the family is reasonably ordinary in terms of wealth and status,' Ronnie explained.

Tia was relaxed by Ronnie's warm, open manner. 'I believe Max is very successful.'

'You know that legendary king who could turn anything to gold with a touch?' Ronnie interposed and nodded solemnly. 'When Max was in banking, he was a total whiz-kid. Doug was always very jealous of him.'

'Who's Doug?'

'A cousin who doesn't visit. He and Max went to the same school but they don't get on,' Ronnie muttered, her face rather flushed as she looked apologetically at Tia. 'Please don't mention to Max that I brought up Doug. I would hate him to think that I was pot-stirring.'

'But why would he think that?' Tia asked in surprise, glancing across the room only to encounter Max's dark observant gaze and experience a snaking shivery little frisson somewhere in the region of her pelvis. She remembered the heat of his mouth and his wickedly skilled hands and was honestly afraid that she could spontaneously combust.

Ronnie winced at the question. 'I'm not getting

into old scandals. The truth is we've always been rather intimidated by Max. When he was younger some of the cousins were quite rude to him because he was related to Andrew's housekeeper. It must've been tough for him. I've never had much time for that kind of snobbery.'

Some of the other guests joined them. Unused to a crowd of strangers, Tia was relieved when Max rescued her to bring her back to her grandfather's side. Seated quietly with the older man, she began to relax again.

Dinner was served in a big dining room at a table almost groaning beneath its weight of crystal, elaborate porcelain and burnished silver.

'It's like another world,' she muttered to Max.

'This lifestyle *does* belong to a bygone age,' Max agreed. 'Andrew lives as his father lived.'

'In incredible comfort,' Tia whispered back. 'But I'd really like to see the housekeeper's flat where you grew up.'

A rueful and surprised smile at that declaration tilted Max's expressive mouth but he had tensed. 'I'm afraid it doesn't exist any more. Andrew renovated the servants' accommodation after my aunt died and upgraded it all.'

'When she did pass away?' Tia asked.

'What was that that you were saying?' her grandfather demanded from her other side.

'I was asking Max how long it is since his aunt died,' Tia explained, looking up.

'Eight years,' Andrew supplied, his thin face tightening. 'It was a complete shock. Carina caught the flu and it turned into pneumonia. She was gone by the time Max managed to get to the hospital.'

'I was a student on a work placement in New York at the time,' Max explained.

'She was a good woman, Max,' the older man pronounced, his voice quavering slightly, his sorrow visible.

And Tia noticed that the table had fallen silent and that the rest of the diners seemed disproportionately interested in the subject being discussed. She wished she had kept quiet and refrained from mentioning Max's aunt, but she could not imagine why the passing of the old man's former housekeeper should rouse such curiosity.

'Tomorrow, I'll show you round the house,' Max murmured lazily, apparently impervious to the tension in the atmosphere. 'Then you'll feel more at home here.'

Tia did not think she could ever feel at home with servants and fancy clothes and even fancier furniture, but then she glanced at Max and a kind of peace entered her soul. He made her feel safe and, while he was present, he made her feel as if she belonged. Yet ironically, if she was to believe Ronnie, as a boy Max had been looked down on at Redbridge for being related to the housekeeper. Was that why he still seemed unapproachable in the company of Andrew's relations and friends? Did he think that old snobbish outlook still existed? Or was it simply that Max was a loner?

After the coffee was served, guests began to leave and a welter of invitations came Tia's way. Her phone was soon crammed with new numbers and names.

'Who's Doug?' Tia pressed Max, recalling Ronnie's nervous backtracking and that evocative word, 'scandal', which had only roused her intense curiosity. 'And why doesn't he visit?'

'One of your cousins. Someone mention him?' Max's strong jaw line squared. 'He doesn't visit because of something that happened a long time ago when we were teenagers,' he admitted grittily. 'It was supposed to destroy my reputation but instead it destroyed Doug's family and made Andrew angry with him.'

Andrew's housekeeper, Janette, a slim, no-nonsense brunette, escorted them upstairs and Tia was forced to swallow back the dozen nosy questions brimming on her lips.

'Mr Grayson asked me to prepare the master suite for you,' the housekeeper informed them.

Max frowned in surprise. 'But that's—' He bit off what he had almost said and compressed his lips. The master suite had once been Andrew's, but since his illness had been diagnosed Andrew had been using a specially adapted room on the ground floor and, given that he needed a wheelchair, it was far more suitable for him. But putting both Max and Tia into the principal room at the hall was making a very public statement about how the owner of the house viewed the status of his newly married granddaughter and her husband.

'I hope you'll be comfortable here, madam,' Janette declared warmly, closing the door on them.

'It's beautiful…' Tia whispered, her bright eyes skimming appreciatively from the welcome log fire burning in the grate to the silk-clad bed and the arrangement of glorious white roses sited in front of the elegantly draped windows. Kicking off her high heels, she moved closer to the fire because the spring chill of an English evening was downright cold compared with the hot, humid climate she was used to.

Turning her head, she focused on Max. 'Now tell me about what happened between you and this Doug,' she urged.

'Later,' Max breathed, his faint accent fracturing the word as his hands came down on her narrow shoulders to slowly turn her round and ease her out of her jacket. The fire cast a reddish glow over her blonde hair, darkening the glossy strands while accentuating the creamy perfection of her skin.

Her breath fluttered in her dry throat. 'Later?' she queried, the evocative scent of him, heat and masculinity with a faint hint of something citrusy, flaring her nostrils.

'Right now I only have time for you,' Max confided, tiny flames reflected from the fire dancing in his dark eyes, transforming them to liquid bronze. 'I let you sleep last night because you were very tired. It was the unselfish thing to do. I also thought you might be...*sore...*'

Her face flamed. 'Not any more.'

'And I need you to be at full strength,' Max imparted, 'because I'm not sure I could be that gentle again, *bella mia*. In your radius I'm in an almost continual state of arousal.'

'Is that so?' Tia almost whispered, all woman, all appreciation of the compliment being paid.

'I'm naturally a selfish bastard but I'm trying very hard to put your needs first.'

Tia lifted her hands and let them skim down over his warm torso, revelling in the strength of the muscular body beneath his shirt. Her fingers drifted lower, discovering the bold outline of him, stroking and caressing with newfound assurance. 'I think you're going to be a terrific husband,' she told him, smiling as he arched his hips into her hand. 'But if we're going to be true equals I've got a lot to learn too.'

'You can practise on me whenever you like,' Max admitted, peeling off his jacket and wrenching at his shirt with flattering impatience.

As the ropes of muscle across his abdomen flexed, Tia unbuckled his belt and unzipped him. Max breathed in starkly, savouring the fact that she constantly took him by surprise. Her hand stroked the length of him and she bent her head, her tongue flicking out to taste him. By the time the warm, wet heat of her mouth engulfed him, Max was almost unbearably full and hard, the grinding pulse of driving hunger gripping him in a vice. Watching her pleasure him excited him beyond bearing and, long before she could tease him to a climax, he reached down and forcefully pulled her up to him, lifting her to plunge his tongue deep into her sweet, intoxicating mouth and feel the answering leap of response vibrate through both of them.

'Max… I—' Tia began.

'Another time,' Max growled, settling her down on the edge of the table by the window, pushing up her skirt and stepping between her spread thighs. '*This* is what I've been dreaming of all day.'

And with that grated confession, Max tilted her back, hurriedly donned a condom and thrust into her hard and deep and strong. The table creaked in complaint but Tia's body was hot and slick with arousal and her tender flesh yielded to him.

*'Dannazione,'* he groaned feverishly. 'You are so tight.'

Tia jerked, her head falling back, blue eyes shaken by his fire as she jerked under him with a helpless moan of sensual pleasure. He was aggressive, dominating in a way he had not been the first time, and the welling of sensation deep within her throbbed with a wild hunger that thrilled her, excitement climbing as his movements became rougher and more demanding. Little internal tremors shimmied through her, bands of tension tightening within her pelvis until her body clenched convulsively around him at the height of her excitement. Wave after glorious wave washed over her as orgasmic aftershocks took her by storm. A low guttural sound was wrenched from him as he too reached completion.

In the aftermath, her body was weighted and limp. Max carried her over to the bed and laid her down, tilting her to unzip her dress and pull it off, unclipping her bra as an afterthought. As he vanished into what was obviously a bathroom, Tia released a happy sigh of contentment. Max had just shown her the hunger, passion and impatience that revealed his need for her. No, there had been nothing lukewarm about that encounter, she reflected with satisfaction, struggling to muster the energy to get up and go and wash.

'Have to take off my make-up,' she mumbled as he stepped out of the shower naked and dripping to reach for a towel.

Tia showered, her feminine core still pulsing from the intensity of the release he had given her and the no less energising discovery that sex could take place on a table as well as a bed and be fast and glorious as well as slow and wonderful.

She padded back to the bed and climbed in, snuggling up to Max without hesitation, one arm wrapping round his broad chest. 'So tell me why this Doug would have wanted to destroy your reputation,' she murmured, curiosity flickering afresh. 'I need to learn all the ins and outs of this family…and the secrets if there are any.'

Max tensed and released his breath in a hiss as he sat up and, in so doing, freed himself from her hold. 'All families have secrets.'

'But this relates to you and we're married,' Tia reminded him unnecessarily.

Max gritted his teeth, belatedly recalling why he never stayed the night with a woman, never risked getting cosy with one, never shared late-night chat sessions. Unfortunately, he acknowledged grimly, there was no escape from a wife occupying the same bed…

# CHAPTER SEVEN

'DOUG AND I attended the same boarding school as teenagers,' Max divulged reluctantly. 'I didn't know him then the way I do now. I trusted him as a friend. It didn't occur to me that he already saw me as competition and thought Andrew took too much interest in me. In my own eyes I was the housekeeper's nephew and I didn't ever expect to be anything more. I was staff, Doug was *family*.'

Tia rested her tousled head back on the pillows and reached for a bronzed masculine hand, lacing her fingers into his without any help from him. 'Go on…'

Max retrieved his hand. 'Doug's family lived nearby and he was a frequent visitor. His mother was on her second marriage and he had a stepsister, a very pretty redhead called Alice. We were only seventeen. Doug brought Alice here repeatedly that summer and I fell in love with her. Only a few weeks after I began seeing her she announced that she was pregnant and that I was the father of her child,' he revealed grittily. 'I was surprised because I had only slept with her on one occasion and I had been… *careful.*'

Tia sat up to study him in consternation. *'And?'* she pressed.

'There was a huge family row. Doug's stepfather stormed over here and tried to beat me up, and then in the midst of all that, with Alice's mother and my aunt screaming in the background and Andrew calling for order, Alice took fright and finally told the truth. The baby was Doug's. She and Doug had been having sex for months and when she realised she was pregnant she panicked because they had been expressly warned by their parents that they were expected to think of each other as brother and sister. Together, she and Doug decided that *I* should be set up to take the blame, which is why she slept with me in the first place…'

'And you loved her,' Tia muttered unevenly, her nails digging into the palms of her hands to enable her to listen to the tawdry tale without making tactless comments. Max had been the fall guy in a nasty set-up, his conviction betrayed by a boy he had believed to be his friend and a girl whom he had learned to care about.

'Yes, but I got over it,' Max completed with a brisk lack of sentiment that did not impress her in the slightest. 'However, Doug's mother and stepfather's marriage broke down because of that pregnancy and, sadly, Alice miscarried a few weeks later, so everyone lost out.'

'At least she told the truth in the end,' Tia sighed.

'Can we please drop the subject now?' Max murmured, his stunning heavily lashed dark eyes welded to her troubled gaze. 'I was a boy and now I'm a man but I still don't like remembering that hellish affair.'

Inside her chest, Tia's heart ached for him and she reached for his hand again.

Max snaked his fingers free a second time. 'You asked me and I told you. I don't need or want your sympathy. It hit me hard at the time because Alice loving me felt special but afterwards I realised it had all been a giant fake. And afterwards, in front of everyone when she was trying to save face and impress Doug, she asked me how I could ever have thought that she could have had feelings for someone like me…'

'Someone like you,' Tia repeated with a frown, rolling over and curving another arm round him, needing to retain some kind of physical contact with him. She was outraged that, not only had the wretched girl tried to set him up, but she had also struck out at his pride with a nasty comment. 'What was that supposed to mean?'

'You don't want to know.'

'No, you don't *want* to tell me,' Tia translated flatly.

'Surely I'm allowed to retain a few secrets,' Max said very drily as he slid free yet again and sprang out of bed. 'If Andrew is still awake I have some business to discuss with him. It slipped my mind earlier.'

'I'm not stupid, Max. If you come back to bed I won't ask any more questions and I won't touch you either,' Tia countered fierily. 'There are only so many times I will allow you to push me away.'

Max set his teeth together, his lean, darkly handsome features clenched hard. 'I know it's a cliché but…it's not you, it's me. I'm not good with demonstrative people. I'm not accustomed to physical affection. The only kind of touching I have ever experienced was sexual and anything else…it feels uncomfortable.'

At least he got back into bed, Tia consoled herself, watching him below her lashes, the strong line of his darkly shadowed jaw line revealing his lingering tension. She stayed on her side of the bed, lying straight, all limbs in alignment like a tomb adornment sculpted out of stone. 'You didn't have affection even when you were a child?' she could not help asking.

'No, and my aunt wasn't the touchy-feely type either.'

'My grandfather?'

'My relationship with Andrew has always been formal.'

And Tia lay there, feeling so sad for him because he had never known normal affection and was now so inhibited that that kind of touch made him uneasy. What must his parents have been like? And why did he never ever mention them? Why had he been left in need of his aunt's care in the first place? That was the crux of the matter, she sensed, but not something she intended to pursue at that moment.

In the morning she woke in Max's arms and she came sleepily awake, moaning involuntarily as expert fingers slid between her parted thighs and played there, sending little ripples of mounting delight filtering through her. Response came as naturally to her as breathing and she arched up as he shifted lithely over her and plunged into her, stretching her with his girth. An almost shocking tide of pleasure engulfed Tia in a blinding surge and she whimpered, eyes fluttering open on his lean dark face and the ravenous dark golden eyes locked to her. And she recognised that in that moment Max was hers, absolutely, unequivocally hers, wanting her, needing her, craving her and that knowledge satisfied the hollow feeling that had spread within her the night before over his disinclination to even hold her close.

He brought her knees up and rocked back into her hard and fast and a fevered gasp escaped her. She couldn't lie still, she couldn't get enough of him and when the voluptuous release of orgasm claimed her she cried out his name. Max rolled over, carrying Tia with him, and slumped back against the pillows. He couldn't keep his hands off her and that bothered him. What about showing a little restraint? A little cool? When he had woken with Tia's shapely little body next to his and the smell of her coconut shampoo surrounding him, he had *had* to have her.

It was that simple, that basic, and no sooner did he reach climax than he was wondering how soon he could have her again. The strength of that lustful craving chilled him to the marrow because it was outside his parameters and like nothing he had ever experienced before.

'Thanks,' Max framed, pausing to drop a kiss on the top of her head and then shifting free of her with alacrity to leave the bed.

*Thanks?* Tia ruminated, savouring the split-second, casual kiss but disappointed by the cut and run that followed. Why had he thanked her? Hadn't she enjoyed herself as much as him? Next time *she* would thank him, she resolved. She could be polite too. In fact she would out-polite him in spades and see how he liked being thanked as if he had provided a service with his body! But what wonderful service he gave, she reflected helplessly.

'What are we doing today?' she asked.

'Apparently you're seeing the family lawyer after breakfast. And no, I don't know what it's about. Andrew doesn't tell me everything,' Max admitted.

A couple of hours later, a little man with an egg-shaped bald head and wire-framed spectacles studied her across Andrew's desk in the library. 'All you have to do is sign these papers,' he told her, fanning out a selection of documents in front of her.

'But what is this about?'

'Your inheritance, of course,' he said in surprise. 'Your grandmother became a wealthy woman during the course of her marriage to Andrew and she left her estate in trust for her grandchildren. You are the *only* grandchild and I am now releasing those funds to you.'

Tia blinked in bewilderment. 'I have an inheritance?' she gulped.

'Now that you're resident in the UK, you do. Your grandmother stipulated that any grandchild had to be resident in this country to qualify, which is why you haven't heard of this bequest before,' he explained patiently.

'How much money is involved in this?' she asked incredulously.

'I haven't had a recent valuation for the jewellery that's included, and of course her bequest is modest in comparison to your grandfather's holdings,' he warned her, 'but I would estimate that her estate is currently worth, well, almost four hundred thousand pounds...'

In shock, Tia froze with the pen in her hand. 'And it's...*mine*?' she exclaimed in disbelief.

'Unconditionally yours,' the older man declared.

Tia signed, stumbling out of the door minutes later to track down Max and tell him that the grandmother she had never met had been kind enough to make her a wealthy woman. Max was infuriatingly unimpressed by that revelation.

'It's *ours* now...that money,' Tia pointed out, trying to win a more enthusiastic response from him. 'Don't you understand that?'

'I have plenty of money of my own,' Max divulged gently, amusement tugging at his beautiful mouth. 'Now thanks to your grandmother you have a nest egg and I'm happy for you.'

Tia calmed down. 'I'd like to make a substantial donation to the convent to help the sisters with their work.'

Max nodded. 'Of course.'

'You don't mind?'

'You can do whatever you like with your inheritance, *bella mia*. While you are with me, however, you will never need to use it,' Max told her smoothly.

'So, what's mine is yours doesn't cut *both* ways?' Tia gathered stiffly.

'I have a visceral need to keep my own wife. Call it the caveman in me,' Max advised.

Tia breathed in deep and slow. They were not going to argue about money. He didn't want what he saw as hers...*fine*! Seemingly he was well enough off to consider her inheritance as a cosy little nest egg barely worthy of excitement. 'And what about when I find a job?'

Max looked at her in astonishment and an eyebrow elevated. 'A *job*?'

'Yes. I haven't decided what I want to do yet but I do want to work. I'm not sure I want to do any more studying though,' she admitted ruefully.

'Take your time and think it over. Andrew supports several charities. Volunteer work could be a practical option for you to begin with,' he suggested.

That night Tia came awake with a start when Max made a sound and she switched on the bedside light, only then registering that he was still asleep and clearly dreaming. The bedding was in a tangle round his long, powerful body, perspiration gleaming on his bronzed skin as he cried out again in Italian and in obvious distress. In dismay she shook his shoulder and voiced his name to waken him.

'You were having a bad dream.'

Max threw himself back against the pillow, breathing rapidly and raking his fingers through his tousled black hair. 'I don't get bad dreams,' he countered defensively.

'You *could* talk to me about it,' Tia told him ruefully, not believing that he didn't get bad dreams for even a second. 'I wouldn't tell anyone else. You can trust me.'

'Leave it, Tia,' Max urged, thinking she would be booking him onto a psychiatric couch if he wasn't careful. 'There will always be stuff in my life that I don't want to discuss.'

Cornflower-blue eyes rested on him with unnerving directness. 'I don't like secrets,' she said simply. 'I want to know everything about you.'

'Good luck with that because I'm not a talker,' Max derided, punching the pillow back into shape and lying back down, making it clear that the conversation was at an end.

Tia lay awake almost until dawn, wondering if she could settle for a husband with secrets. She didn't think she could. She hadn't been joking or exaggerating when she had admitted to wanting to know all that there was to know about him. On her terms, that kind of fearless honesty was the backbone of a strong relationship, but Max didn't seem to crave that kind of closeness and it worried her.

'And *this* is what you're wearing tonight?' Ronnie gasped in admiration as Tia brought the long ice-blue gown out to show her friend. The fabric shimmered as if it were sprinkled with diamonds. 'Tia… it's gorgeous!'

Grayson Industries had started out fifty years earlier and a half-century party was being staged in a luxury London hotel as a celebration. Tia was accompanying Andrew and Max and finally stepping out in public as a Grayson.

'And it's blue because Max likes me in blue,' Tia muttered shamefacedly as Teddy capered round her feet, getting in the way.

The little terrier had been much quieter since he'd emerged from quarantine and was no longer so aggressive. He behaved like Tia's shadow now though, as if he was afraid that she might disappear again.

Ronnie shook her dark head. 'You are *such* a newly-wed. And Max isn't missing the single life, is he? There he is with an apartment in London and he still flies back here every night to be with you.'

Tia was more inclined to put Max's frequent flying down to his fondness for her grandfather. Unfortunately, she was still feeling very guilty about the discreet visit she had made to the doctor first thing that morning, because she hadn't been able to bring herself to admit that she believed she needed a pregnancy test to Max or to anyone else. Somehow that little worry had become her secret. And now that little worry had grown into a *massive* worry…

But, she didn't have to share *everything* with Max, did she? It nagged at her conscience that only a few months ago she had thought less of Max for his unwillingness to share everything and now here she was doing the exact same thing. But then, no doubt like Max, she had her reasons.

And now that she knew that she *was* pregnant she felt stupid for having been so blind because she had always assumed that a woman ought to somehow know such a thing even if the signs beforehand were misleading. They had been married for three months and she had twice had what she believed to be periods. Admittedly both had been unusually irregular and brief, but when she'd told Max that she was out of commission he had smiled and laughed, pointing out that they now had the proof that she wasn't pregnant. And fool that she was, she had believed that Max must know the symptoms of pregnancy better than she did. When her appetite had failed, when her breasts had become swollen and she had suffered strange moments of dizziness, she had ignored those sensations until she became worried enough to consult a doctor.

Consequently, Tia had been shattered when the doctor had told her that there was nothing actually wrong with her and she was merely suffering the common side effects of early pregnancy. Apparently her experience of partial periods was not quite as unusual as she had assumed, nor was it a sign that her pregnancy was unstable. But how was she supposed to tell Max that she was pregnant now when he was totally unprepared for that reality? His relief at the seeming proof that she was not pregnant some weeks after their wedding loomed large in her memory. Max had been relieved that she had not conceived and had felt free to reveal that reality.

Was it any wonder that she had not even told him that she'd intended to visit a doctor? Unsure of how he would react to her secret fear, she had refused to admit her apprehension. In truth, things had been so good between them that she hadn't wanted to risk tipping the scales by sharing a worry that had seemed groundless.

Yet in spite of her concern, being married to Max did make her incredibly happy. Oh, nothing was perfect, Tia conceded. He worked too many hours and he could be so preoccupied with business matters that he didn't always hear what she said. He commuted daily by helicopter between the London headquarters of Grayson Industries and Redbridge Hall. Max hadn't dared say it but she knew that he didn't want her to find a job and for the moment she had put that ambition on hold because learning that her grandfather was living on borrowed time had changed her outlook.

Andrew had only months, not years, ahead of him and she was keen to make the most of what time he had left. She had been devastated when he'd finally confessed that he was terminally ill and initially angry with Max for not telling her sooner, but she had gradually come to understand that Andrew had wanted her homecoming to be a joyous occasion unclouded by anything distressing.

Tia also understood that it was the very strength of her feelings for Max that had enabled her to adapt to the awareness that her grandfather would not be in her life for much longer. Without Max's support she would have been far more devastated at the prospect of that coming loss. In truth, she didn't know when she had fallen for Max because he had been so very important to her from the first moment she had laid eyes on him. His first look, his first smile, his first kiss? It was as if he had cast a spell on her and bound her to him bone and sinew.

At the same time, Tia was painfully aware that Max didn't love her back. Maybe she wasn't the sort of woman who appealed to him on that higher level, she sometimes thought ruefully. In any case, Max kept his own emotions in check as if he feared them and she could hardly credit that he had decided love was not for him based on a distraught teenage girl's betrayal. Didn't he realise that everyone got hurt at some stage when it came to love?

Tia had loved her father long and undeservedly despite his cutting criticisms and lack of interest in her. She loved Max because he made her feel as though everything he did was for her benefit, whether it was asking Andrew's cook to surprise her with a Brazilian meal or coming home with random little gifts for her that he just so happened to have stumbled on. A handbag the same colour as her eyes? A book he thought she might enjoy? A pendant with ninety-odd sparkling diamonds denoting the number of days they had been married? Max did nothing by halves and he took being a husband seriously. How could she fairly ask for more than that? How could she reasonably expect more from a man who had only proposed to her in the first place because there was a risk he could have got her pregnant?

And yet, unreasonable or not, Tia recognised that she had a very strong need to be loved. And for a husband whom she could confide anything in at any time. But Max's very unwillingness to commit himself to that level of frankness had put barriers up between them and made Tia less open to sharing her own private insecurities and worries. Her parents' lack of love had left her vulnerable and she suspected that Max had had a similar experience with his parents. Unfortunately, that same lack had left Tia craving love to feel secure while it had left Max denying his need for it and shutting the possibility out as being too risky.

Tia knew that she should not allow Max's lack of

enthusiasm for having a child to influence her thinking. But that was impossible, she thought unhappily. She knew she would prefer to have a family while she was still young but still wondered if being older would make her a *better* parent. Reminding herself that she could not do worse than her own parents had done with her, Tia swallowed hard. What sort of a mother would she be? Hopefully a better one than her own had been. But what if Inez's inability to love Tia enough to keep her had been passed on to Tia? She shivered at that fear and prayed that she would be able to love her child like any normal mother.

But most daunting of all, what was she going to do if the man she loved genuinely didn't *want* their baby? Fearful of that pessimistic worry taking control of her before she even had the chance to break that news to Max, Tia thrust it to the back of her mind and suppressed it hard.

She was hopelessly excited about the baby she carried, she conceded ruefully, daring to hope that, once Max got over the shock of her condition, he would feel the same. But starting a family *was* a life-altering event, she conceded afresh, and anxiety gripped her. She was only just learning how to live in the modern world and soon she would be responsible for guiding an innocent child through the same process. But she would have Max with her, she told herself urgently. Max had been everywhere, done everything. Max was her failsafe go-to whenever she needed help. But that made her dependent on him and she hated that reality because she didn't think it was healthy for her to be forced to continually look to him for advice. It made her feel more like a child than an adult and she badly wanted to stand on her own feet. And sadly, she appreciated, a pregnancy was only going to make independence even more of an impossible challenge.

'You look stunning,' her grandfather told her warmly that evening as she climbed out of the limousine, hovering in spite of his objections while he was assisted from the vehicle at the side entrance to the big hotel.

Max had opted to stay in the city and change at his apartment before meeting them. He emerged to greet them, wonderfully tall, sleek and sophisticated in a dinner jacket and narrow black trousers that provided the ultimate presentation for his wide-shouldered, narrow-hipped, long-legged frame. Her breath snarled in her throat, familiar damp heat licking at the heart of her, as always her body and her senses clamouring on every level for Max's attention. Sometimes she suspected that she was a shamelessly sexual woman and her colour rose as her eyes met the dark allure of his, her spine tingling as though he had touched her.

And then the moment was gone as one of the paparazzi who had been waiting in a clump at the front entrance came running to snatch a photo and, with

Andrew's nurse taking charge of the wheelchair, they hurried into the hotel.

'That dress is sensational on you,' Max husked, gazing down at her with hot dark eyes, the pulse at his groin a deeply unwelcome reminder of his susceptibility to his bride.

He needed to pull back from Tia; he knew that. He knew that he needed to pull back and give her space. In a few months' time without Andrew around Tia might decide she wanted her freedom and there would be little point him craving then what he could no longer have. Was that why he had to have her every night? Why going one night without her felt like deprivation of the worst kind? Her hunger matched his though, he reminded himself stubbornly. The need was mutual. And being hooked on sex wasn't that dangerous a weakness, was it?

Tia caught at his sleeve. 'I have something to tell you,' she whispered, needing to share, wanting him to demonstrate the same joy that had been growing in her since she'd first learned that she was carrying their first child.

She had wasted so much energy tormenting herself with doubts and insecurities while all the time her deep abiding pleasure at the prospect of becoming a mother was quietly building on another level. She was going to have Max's baby and she was happy about that development and, now that the opportunity had come, she suddenly couldn't wait to share her news.

'We've got official photos first,' Max warned her.

So, they posed and smiled with Andrew to mark the occasion and then, Andrew safely stowed in the company of old friends, Max began to introduce her to what felt like hundreds of people. She set her champagne glass down and quietly asked the waiter for a soft drink while she waited for her moment to tell Max about their child.

The moment came during a lull in the music when everybody was standing around chatting and, for the first time, they were miraculously alone. 'Remember I said I had something to tell you?' Tia whispered.

Lashes as dark and lustrous as black lace lifted on level dark golden eyes and he lifted his chin in casual acknowledgment. 'I'm listening.'

'I'm pregnant,' Tia told him baldly.

And beneath her gaze Max turned paper pale below his bronzed skin, his facial muscles jerking taut to throw his hard bone structure into shocking prominence. 'Are you serious?' he pressed in disbelief. 'How can you be? You were clear—'

'No. We thought I was and we were wrong.'

Max was shattered and struggling to hide the fact. She had conceived? Although his brain knew better, he had always subconsciously supposed that a pregnancy was unlikely after a single sexual encounter. He had simply assumed it wasn't going to happen, had been convinced by the evidence that they were safe from that threat and he had relaxed. And now that she was cheerfully assuring him that it *had* happened he had no prepared strategy of how to behave to fall back on in his hour of need. And it *was* his hour of need, Max registered sickly as an image of his thuggish father's face swam before his eyes and momentarily bereft him of breath. Like a punch in the gut, he had once seen his father's hated image every time he closed his eyes to go to sleep, his father, his bogeyman, the memory of brutality that had haunted him since the dreadful night his mother had died.

'But you can't be sure yet,' Max assumed, grasping hopefully at straws. 'Surely it's too soon to be sure? You'll have to see a doctor.'

'I saw a doctor this morning. It's official. I'm pregnant. For goodness' sake, it seems I've been pregnant all along,' she divulged shakily. 'We'll be parents in six months' time.'

Tia felt so sick because Max wasn't a very good actor. He was appalled by the idea of her being pregnant and he couldn't hide it. A tight band of pain seized her chest and she could hardly breathe for hurt and disillusionment. How could she have been so naïve as to credit that Max would welcome a baby that would undoubtedly disrupt his life even more than she had done? Max had given up his freedom to marry her and possibly he had hoped that he would eventually regain that freedom, but the birth of a child would make that process a great deal more complicated.

Max released his breath in a rush. 'You took me by surprise.'

'Obviously,' Tia pronounced tightly, focusing fixedly on his scarlet silk tie, refusing to meet his eyes and see anything else she didn't want to see because it hurt too much.

Yes, she had accepted that he wasn't in love with her, but she had trustingly believed that he would welcome fatherhood even if the planning or the timing weren't quite ideal. But that had been a false hope because she had judged Max all wrong. Max just didn't *want* a child, which was a much more basic issue. Suddenly she was in a situation she had never ever envisaged and flinching in horror from the ramifications of what she was discovering. How could she possibly stay married to a man who didn't want their child?

Even her own parents had not been that set against becoming parents. Her father would have been quite content to be a father if her mother had stuck around to take care of her, while her mother had been content to be a mother as long as her husband was a wealthy businessman based in London. When Paul Grayson had announced his plans to become a missionary and work in some of the poorest places on earth, Tia's mother had been aghast and the baby she'd carried had simply become an inconvenient burden tying her down to a life she had very quickly learned to loathe.

'We'll discuss this later,' Max breathed in a driven undertone. 'Discuss how to handle it.'

*Handle it?* What did he mean by that? And what was there to discuss? A pregnancy didn't come with choices as far as Tia was concerned. A cold shiver snaked down her spine as Max turned to address a man who had hailed him. Was he hinting at the possibility of a termination? Surely he could not credit that she would even consider such an option?

The evening wore on with Tia seeking out her grandfather's company and sitting with a group of much older men. But she remained hyper-aware of Max's every move and glance in her direction. He looked forbidding, his high cheekbones taut, his beautiful mouth compressed. It struck her as a savage irony that Max should seem as unhappy as she was and that that reality could only drive them further apart. He should have been more honest with her when he proposed, she thought bitterly. He should have admitted then that he didn't want a child in his life. He had been prepared to marry her to throw a mantle of respectability over the possibility that she might be pregnant, but evidently even then he must have been hoping that she would fail to conceive.

Shortly before they left because Andrew was grey with exhaustion, her grandfather gripped her hand firmly in his. 'Do you have any idea how much I regret not standing up to my son when he put you into that convent?'

'It was his decision, not yours,' she responded gently.

'I should've fought him, offered him money for his good works in return for you,' Andrew sighed wearily. 'But he was my son and I wanted him to come home and I was afraid to take the risk of arguing with him.'

'I was fine at the convent. I *am* fine,' Tia pointed out quietly.

'You're a wonderful girl,' Andrew assured her as they waited indoors for the limousine to arrive.

'And I have a little secret to tell you,' Tia whispered, suddenly desperate to give her news to someone who would appreciate it.

Her grandfather responded to her little announcement with a huge smile and he squeezed her hand with tears glistening in his blue eyes. 'Wonderful,' was all he could say. *'Wonderful.'*

'Congratulations,' Andrew told Max when he swung into the car with them. 'Our family will continue into another generation.'

For once Max experienced no inner warmth at being included in Andrew's family and his lean, strong face remained taut, his hard jaw line clenched. He was furious with himself. He knew his lack of enthusiasm had hurt and distressed Tia. He had allowed his emotions to control him, filling him with a fearful sense of insecurity. *Man up,* his intelligence urged him with derision. *Be an optimist, not a pessimist.* If he put his mind to it, surely he was capable of being a good father?

'I'm very tired,' Tia admitted at the foot of the stairs. 'Perhaps we could talk tomorrow.'

'You go on up to bed,' her grandfather urged

cheerfully. 'Max and I will have a nightcap to celebrate.'

'You're not supposed—' she began.

'One drink,' Andrew specified with a wry grin. 'Surely even the doctor would not deny me that on a special occasion?'

Tia mounted the stairs, striving not to relive Max's reaction to her pregnancy. She fingered her pendant with its ninety-odd diamonds as she removed her jewellery. A diamond for every day she and Max had been together. She had thought that that was so romantic but obviously it had just been a gesture, the sort of gesture a man made when he wanted to look like a devoted new husband. That newly acquired cynicism shocked her, but what else was she to think?

Tia clambered into bed and, in spite of her unhappy thoughts, discovered that she was much too tired to lie awake. She slept, waking as dawn light broke through the curtains to find Max shaking her shoulder.

Max gripped her hand, which struck her as strange and she frowned up at him. 'What's wrong?' she framed.

'You have to be very brave,' he breathed with a ragged edge to his dark deep voice.

Tears were shimmering in his liquid dark eyes and that fast, she knew. *'Andrew?'* she exclaimed.

'He passed away in his sleep during the night. A fatal heart attack. I'm sorry, Tia…'

A sob formed in Tia's tight throat. She didn't think

she could bear the pain. Max and Andrew together had been her support system but Max had let her down the night before and now Andrew was gone as well. In a world that now seemed grey, she wondered how she could go on and then she remembered her baby and knew that she had more strength than she had ever given herself credit for.

# CHAPTER EIGHT

TIA SAW HER MOTHER, Inez, seated inside the church and almost stumbled on the way to the front pew.

'What is it?' Max murmured.

'My mother's here,' she framed, dry-mouthed.

'Well, Andrew was her father-in-law for a while,' Max conceded. 'Perhaps she felt a need to pay her respects.'

But the former Inez Grayson, now Inez Santos, was not a religious, respectful nor, for that matter, a sentimental woman. And her presence at Andrew's funeral shook her daughter, who had not seen her parent in almost ten years. The past few days had turned into a roller coaster of grief, disbelief and anger for Tia. Max had kept his distance, using another bedroom after telling her that he didn't want to 'disturb' her. Tia had run the gamut of frightening insecurities. Was her pregnancy such a turn-off that he didn't want to be physically close to her any longer? Or did Max need privacy to come to terms with his own grief at the loss of the man who had done so much to support him when he was young and vulnerable? And, moreover, who had expressed his confidence in Max to the extent of making him CEO of one of the largest business concerns in the UK.

It would be typical of Max to choose not to *share* that grief with her. He was much more likely than she was to wall up his feelings and hide them, particularly when he was already very much aware that he was not actually related to his former mentor except by marriage. It hurt her that yet another event that she felt should have brought them closer had in fact driven them further apart. They had both fondly trusted that Andrew would be spared to them for another few months and unhappily they had learned that no timer could be set on death. Her grandfather's heart had given out under the strain of his illness and that was God's will, Tia reminded herself, and she would not question that.

'The minute I heard I dropped everything to come to you!' Inez gushed as she intercepted Tia on the church steps. 'You need your *mamae* now more than ever.'

'Your maternal concern comes a little late in the day,' Max murmured with lethal cool.

As a muscle pulled tight on Inez's perfectly made up and undeniably exquisite face, guilt assailed Tia because, for the first time, her mother looked her almost fifty years. 'You're welcome back at the house,' she forced herself to declare.

'Why did you invite her?' Max asked drily as soon as they were back in the limousine. 'You know Cable's waiting to read Andrew's will and she can't be present for that.'

'Inez can mingle with the other guests,' Tia retorted. 'Whatever else she is, she's still my mother. I should respect that.'

And not for the first time, Tia resented the reality that the funeral had been rushed to facilitate the will reading because the stability of her grandfather's business empire depended on smooth continuity being re-established as soon as was humanly possible. It was all to do with stocks and shares, she recalled numbly, the weariness of stress and early pregnancy tugging at her again.

She took her seat in the library with Andrew's other relatives for the reading of the will. The lawyer read out bequests to long-serving staff first before moving on to the children of Tia's grandmother's siblings. Disappointment then flashed across a lot of faces and Tia stopped looking, thinking that people probably always hoped for more than they received in such cases and, mindful of her own inheritance, she was determined not to be judgemental. Silence fell as Mr Cable moved on to the main body of the will and the disposition of Andrew's great wealth.

Redbridge Hall and its contents were left in perpetuity to Tia and any children she might have, along with sufficient funds to ensure its maintenance and a sizeable private income for her support, but the bulk of Andrew's money and his business holdings were left exclusively to Max. Only if Tia and Max divorced would there be any change in that status quo and, even then, Max would have the final word on every decision taken in that situation.

A shocked muttering burst out amongst Tia's companions as a wave of dissension ran around the room. Tia was disconcerted by the will but not surprised, having long since recognised that her grandfather's strongest desire had always been to ensure that Grayson Industries survived for future generations. Building Grayson Industries into an international empire had been Andrew's life's work, after all, and, as far as Tia could see, how he chose to dispose of his life's work and earnings had been entirely his business.

As threats to take the will to court and distasteful insinuations and accusations about Andrew's state of mind and undue influence being used on him were uttered, the lawyer mentioned that Andrew had taken the precaution of having a psychiatric report done a couple of months earlier to make bringing a court case on such grounds virtually impossible. He also intimated that his employer had for several years been very frank about his hope that Max would marry his granddaughter and take permanent charge of his empire. Amidst much vocal bad feeling, Tia rose from her seat and quite deliberately closed her hand round Max's, for as far as she was concerned Andrew's last wishes were sacrosanct and she did not want anyone to think that she stood anywhere but on Max's side of the fence.

Not that Max, his dark head held high as they left the library, seemed to be in need of her support, particularly not when those also present at the will reading spread amongst the other guests. A low, intent murmur of chatter soon sounded around them and Tia could tell that she and Max were the centre of attention. Her face went pink at that acknowledgement but Max seemed gloriously impervious to the interest of other people.

'How do you feel about all this?' Max enquired almost lazily.

'Andrew *wanted* you to inherit,' Tia murmured with quiet emphasis. 'It was his business and it was his right to dispose of it as he saw fit.'

His lean, strong profile taut, Max dealt her a frowning appraisal from glittering dark deep-set eyes as if questioning that she could really feel like that. Tia evaded his direct gaze because what had happened between them in Brazil was playing heavily on her mind and she knew she had questions to ask her husband before she was willing to bury the subject.

'We'll talk in here.' Max flung open a door off the crowded drawing room. 'By the way, don't feel sorry for your cousins. Andrew made generous settlements on all of them *before* he died.'

'Good to know.' Tia preceded him into a small sitting room. Faded curtains and rather outmoded furniture attested to the fact that it had once been her grandmother's favourite room. It had stayed unchanged for over a quarter of a century and the sight of it and the beautiful view out over the colourful rose garden never failed to touch Tia's heart. Her grandfather had mentioned how he still liked to picture her grandmother sitting writing letters at her bureau and of how in the initial stages of his grief he had liked to sit there to feel close to her again.

'How do you feel?' Max prompted again, standing with wide shoulders angled back and legs braced as if he expected her to attack. 'You can be honest… tell me.'

'Did you know?' Tia asked hesitantly, her luminous gaze welded to his devastatingly handsome, lean dark features.

'What would be in the will? Andrew filled me in on the details only *after* we had married,' Max admitted flatly, raking a frustrated hand through his tousled black hair. 'Prior to that I assumed he would leave it all jointly to both of us.'

The will had shaken Max and it was ironic that, while the disposal of Andrew's assets had made Andrew's other relatives jealous, it had almost made Max groan. He didn't need the ownership of Grayson Industries to feel good about himself or the future. As far as Max was concerned, Grayson Industries would always rightfully belong to Tia, who was a Grayson by birth. He was not sorry, though, to be left with complete autonomy over the business because he would not have enjoyed interference from any other source.

But what Max disliked most of all was the suspicion that Andrew's will had muddied the water in his marriage and no matter what Tia said, she had to have serious doubts about how much she could trust him now. Did she secretly suspect that he had married her for her money? He needed to be more frank with her about *why* he was with her and why he had been willing to marry her, he acknowledged grudgingly.

The worst of Tia's tension had already dissipated. 'It would never occur to me to think of you as a fortune hunter, Max,' she confided ruefully. 'I would never think that of you.'

'Then possibly you should think again. I have to tell you the truth because I won't lie about it. Before I came out to Brazil to collect you, Andrew told me how worried he was about bringing you home here when he was dying. He was worried sick about how you would cope as his heiress in a world so far removed from that of the convent and he *asked* me to marry you to protect you.'

All her natural colour draining away in the face of that unwelcome revelation, Tia fell back a step from him in consternation: Max had not freely chosen to be with her. It was as though her whole world lurched and spun around her because she suddenly felt sick and dizzy and disorientated. Her legs like woolly supports, she dropped down heavily into an armchair and stared back up at him, her cornflower-blue eyes huge in the white triangle of her face.

'That is the one secret I won't keep from you, *bella mia*,' Max declared harshly. 'Andrew came up with the original idea. You heard the family lawyer refer to it. It was news to me, however, that he was considering the idea years before he mentioned it to me. I said I'd consider it after I had met you but the minute I saw you, I stopped considering anything. I wanted you and I didn't want any other man to have you.'

Tia gazed back at him in shock, never having associated such strong emotions with Max.

'Right there and then, I became determined that you would be mine,' Max continued in a harsh undertone. 'I didn't think about the business or the money. That didn't come into it for me. I'm an ambitious man but prior to meeting you I had built up enough wealth to satisfy me and anything more was icing on the cake. Somehow in a very short space of time you became both the icing *and* the cake. Even so, I was intolerably greedy and selfish. I didn't want any other man to have an excuse to come near you.'

'Intolerably?' Tia queried his choice of words shakily.

'A more honourable man would have wanted you to come home and have the freedom to explore the dating scene. My blood ran cold at that prospect. I'm possessive. I didn't want to run the risk of losing you to someone else. I didn't want anyone to have the chance to take you from me. I knew I would meet Andrew's expectations and look after you and, whatever happens, I will continue to do so. When I give my word, I stand by it, and you are my wife and I will always stand by that.'

And she recognised that stubborn strength and resolution in him and it cut her and made her bleed where it didn't show, made her bleed for what she couldn't have and what she would have given anything to possess. Had he loved her she would have forgiven him anything but he didn't *love* her. He desired her. Yes, she understood that perfectly, for she had desired him with equal fervour when they had first met. But desire had steadily transformed into love where she was concerned, only it hadn't happened that way for Max. She understood that he would do only right by her; that she could rely on him and that he had not married her only for the riches that that marriage would bring him.

But, that didn't change the reality that she was married to Max now because *Andrew* had wanted Max to be with her, giving her the protection that Andrew had known he would not be around for long to give. Their sexual chemistry had persuaded Max that such a marriage could work but without the pressure of her grandfather's emotional blackmail would it have ever occurred to Max to marry her?

Tia thought not. Furthermore, there was a huge unacknowledged elephant in the room—the baby Max had yet to mention in any shape or form. He had had three days to brood. Surely that was time enough for a man to deal with an unexpected and unwelcome development? And as Tia rested troubled eyes on Max, her heart was sinking because she knew they did not have a future together. He didn't want their child. He would do what he had to do, say what he had to say but without the spur of love and genuine interest he would be a poor parent. Much as her own father had been, Tia decided wretchedly, bad memories pulling at her. She had spent a lifetime trying to please a man who could not be pleased. She had struggled endlessly to win his love and approval, writing him weekly letters to which he never responded and passing every exam that came her way. And her efforts had only been a thankless and heartbreaking learning experience and she would never impose that burden on her baby. Sometimes, she thought sadly, *no* father could be better than an uncaring, indifferent one.

'Now isn't the time for this,' she breathed, rising with sudden decisiveness. 'We have a house full of visitors.'

And Max thought, so much for the much-vaunted tactic of telling the truth and baring your heart. It hadn't got him anywhere. Tia's face was shuttered, eyes on lockdown, her lush mouth closed. *Madonna diavolo!* He wasn't going to lose her—no way was he prepared to let her go! Particularly not now when she was carrying his child. *His* child, he reminded himself doggedly, striving valiantly to accustom himself to that astonishing idea. Some time soon when her grief was not so fresh he would tell her the whole story of his childhood and then she would understand his apprehension, wouldn't she?

Right now he didn't want to weigh her down with any more stress and worry. She looked fragile as a bird in her elegant black dress and he knew she was eating little more than a sparrow's ration at mealtimes. The tension of anxiety settled into Max's bones. So far he was dismayed by what pregnancy appeared to be doing to his wife. He knew that a pregnancy wasn't an illness but Tia looked wan, thin and drained and her once buoyant spirits were at basement level.

Tia quickly discovered that gossiping tongues had been busy in the drawing room because her mother wasted no time in tracking her down to draw her into a quiet corner and say angrily, 'We'll take Andrew's will to court. It's a disgrace. Your inheritance has been stolen by your husband. He's a fortune hunter! No wonder he doesn't want me around!'

'I'm not taking anyone to court, Inez,' Tia countered in a firm undertone.

'Can't you call me Mamae like my other children?' the blonde woman asked plaintively.

Tia breathed in deep. 'I don't want to be unkind but you were never my mother in the way you were a mother to them…and it's too late now. We're strangers. I needed a mother when I was a little girl. I've got used to not having one now.'

'But it could be different...if I stayed here, if I *lived* with you,' Inez argued vehemently, 'then we could get to know each other.'

'*Lived* with me? Why would you want to live with me when your home and your husband are in Brazil?' Tia queried in genuine astonishment.

'Francisco has replaced me with a younger woman,' Inez admitted with a dismissive toss of her head and a shrug. 'We're currently going through a divorce and my children have elected to stay with their father and their future stepmother.'

Tia had a scornful urge to ask her mother what it felt like to be abandoned and was immediately deeply ashamed of that spiteful prompting. 'I'm sorry. It must be very hard for you right now.'

'But if I could move in with you, everything would be much easier,' Inez confessed. 'I would have no financial worries and I could live in comfort.'

And comprehension set in then with Tia. Her mother had only come to the funeral because she had decided that Tia might finally be useful to her, and of course she wanted Tia to take Max to court and fight Andrew's will because the wealthier Tia was, the more useful she could be to her mother. Bitterness threatened to claim Tia. For an instant, she recalled the loneliness of convent life for a little girl who never got to go home to a family during the holidays like her classmates. Inez's self-interest was not a surprise but what did surprise Tia was that her mother's selfishness could still hurt and disappoint her.

'That's not possible,' Tia responded deflatingly.

'But this is *your* house now,' Inez protested, making it clear that she had received that confidential information from someone present at the reading of the will. 'You can have whoever you like to stay and who better than your mother?'

'Her husband,' another voice interposed and Tia glanced up in dismay to find Max towering over them, his lean, strong face formidable in its hard resolve. 'Tia has me and right now she doesn't need anyone else.'

Inez's mouth took on a venomous twist but before she could say anything more, Tia stepped away. 'It was good to see you today, Inez,' she said politely as she walked away.

'I feel awful,' she whispered to Max. 'I don't feel anything for her. Well, actually, that's another lie. At one point I felt angry, bitter and nasty and I hate feeling like that.'

Max shrugged a broad shoulder. 'She made it that way when she walked out on you and never came back, *bella mia*. Don't blame yourself for being human.'

And instantly, Tia felt soothed, gazing up into lustrous dark golden eyes, her tummy flipping a somersault in sudden excitement as that sliding sensation thrummed between her legs and she ached down deep inside. Every response seemed heightened by the rawness of her turbulent emotions. For a heady split second she craved his mouth with every fibre of her being, hunger threatening to roar up inside her like a raging fire. She sucked in a shuddering breath to calm her fevered body, wondering where she would focus that passion when she no longer had Max. On her baby? On some other interest?

Max swallowed with difficulty, his hand clenching into a fist and digging into his pocket. It was neither the time nor the place and her fine-boned face was etched with strain and fatigue. He didn't want her to have to play hostess any longer; he wanted to scoop her up in his arms and lay her down to rest somewhere quiet and peaceful. Knowing she would do her duty, however, he stayed by her side, handling the more difficult conversations that roused her grief and brought tears to her eyes. He urged her to sit down whenever possible and was barely able to conceal his relief when people began leaving.

'I think I'll have an early night,' Tia told him over a dinner in which she merely rearranged her food on her plate.

'Good idea. It's been a very long day.'

'I miss him,' Tia confessed gruffly.

'I've never been in this house before when he wasn't here. It feels strange.'

Tia lay in the bath, composing herself while she made plans for her future. Max didn't want their child and he didn't want her except in the most basic sexual way. She deserved better and she wasn't about to settle for less, she told herself urgently. She had to be strong and decisive. She would leave and use her grandmother's inheritance to build a new independent life, possibly the life she would have enjoyed had she not met Max. What else could she do?

Max had married her primarily to please Andrew and Andrew was no longer alive to be hurt and disappointed by her decision to abandon her hasty marriage. Max wouldn't miss her. He would be far too busy with Grayson Industries. He didn't want their child, couldn't even bring himself to talk about the baby she carried. No, the best he could seem to do was ignore the subject in its entirety. Leaving was her only option.

Max would not feel he had lost out when he had no contact with the child he had accidentally fathered. Their child would lose out on having a father but if Max wasn't keen on being a father, wouldn't his absence be less damaging in the long run? Perhaps years from now Max would succumb to curiosity as her own mother once had and he would find that he could communicate more easily with their child when he or she was more mature. Tia knew she could not expect to stay hidden for ever.

Tears dampened her cheeks in the hothouse temperature of the opulent bathroom. How could she walk away from the man she loved? Even if it was the best thing for them both? Eventually they would have to get a divorce, which would leave them free to seek another relationship. Just then Tia didn't think she would ever again be attracted to anyone and the thought of Max with anyone else absolutely destroyed her. Indeed, all she could think of at that instant was Max, his hair-roughened bronzed skin hot and a mixture of rough and smooth against her, the intoxicating taste of him, the burning need he excited…

Irritated with herself, Tia clambered out of the bath, her body tingling and pulsing, and wrapped herself in a towel. In the bedroom, she hovered. One last night, she thought crazily, one last night with Max…why not? Why the heck not? She loved him, she wanted him. Afterwards she would write him a letter explaining how she felt but she wouldn't tell him everything. If she told him she loved him he would feel guilty that he had hurt her. No, she would tell him that she needed her freedom; that life was too short to waste, that setting out to make her own life and live alone was what she had always dreamt of…and it would be the truth with just a few salient facts withheld.

Swathed in a towelling robe, she walked out into the corridor and down to the bedroom that she knew Max was using. She didn't knock on the door because she felt that would be silly. No, she walked straight in and caught Max lying in his boxers on the bed watching the business news. Against the backdrop of the white linen sheets, he was a breathtaking vision of masculine perfection.

'I don't want to be alone tonight,' she told him honestly.

Max was very much taken aback. He sat up, brilliant dark eyes widening as Tia untied the sash of the robe and let the robe tumble in a heap to the floor. He couldn't believe what he was witnessing because Tia was usually endearingly modest and now here she was naked under the lights. Yet light was a good friend to that porcelain skin with its pearlised glow, that honey-blonde hair as glossy as polished silk and the full, pouting, pink-tipped breasts that shifted with her every movement. Max had never liked surprises but just then he felt as if he had died and gone to heaven and the television went silent as soon as he had made a successful fumbling attempt to locate the remote.

'I'm all yours, *bella mia*,' he breathed thickly, the pulse at his groin responding with alarming rapidity to his appreciation of her.

Tia got on the bed and slid over him like a siren, leaning down, pink-tipped breasts brushing his chest as she planted her succulent pink lips against his. Max put his hands up and dragged her down to him, his urgency thrilling her. Bossy as always, he rearranged her to his satisfaction on the bed and worked his sensual passage down over her squirming body from her delicate collarbone to her straining nipples and then all the way down to the tender flesh between her thighs.

'I wanted to torture you,' she complained. 'This was supposed to be *my* show.'

'Some other time,' Max growled, fighting to stay in control as he teased her damp receptive core and she made little gasping sounds that went straight to his groin and made him as rigid and hard as steel.

'When's it going to be my turn?' she complained, running a desperate hand down over his strong muscular shoulders and clawing her fingers through his hair because those were the only parts of him she could reach.

'I'm in no condition to argue right now.'

He turned her firmly over onto her knees and plunged with erotic force into her. She cried out because he felt so impossibly good and she was only just realising in sudden dismay that if everything went to plan she would never experience such intimacy with Max again. That conviction panicked her and his next surge only intensified her body's reaction. She arched as the tingling waves of excitement threatened to consume her, her whole body hot and liquid with uncontrollable craving.

'Don't you dare stop!' she moaned, barely knowing what she was saying, unable to think and too frightened by what she had thought to even want to think.

And Max didn't. The long dreadful day of sadness faded with every voluptuously satisfying penetration of her receptive body. Tia's need for him had startled him because her muted response to his earlier explanation about how he felt about her had disappointed him. Their all-consuming passion sparked and flamed into a frantic blaze of hunger neither of them could restrain. As release claimed them both into the trembling, perspiring aftermath, Max groaned out something ragged in Italian.

When Tia rolled away, Max stretched out an arm and brought her back to him, knowing she needed that closeness, fighting his own awkwardness to give her what she deserved. He had not enjoyed sleeping apart from her, but it had been a necessary sacrifice when Andrew's death had brought her so low, when he couldn't trust himself to share a bed with her and not reach for her in the night.

'Thank you,' she said softly. 'That was amazing.'

'You don't ever need to thank me for something that gives me so much pleasure.'

'You thanked me once,' she reminded him.

Max didn't remember. '*Did* I?'

'You did,' she whispered, quietly pulling free to slip out of the bed, knowing she had that letter to write and plans to make.

'I got it wrong,' Max husked softly. 'Sometimes I'm going to get it wrong without meaning to.'

Tia's eyes prickled with tears because there was just no room for getting it wrong with a baby. It had gone wrong for her and she suspected it had gone wrong for Max as well, because why else would he be so reluctant to talk about his childhood? But she was determined not to let it go wrong for her child even if that entailed walking out on the man she loved. Her child was not going to pay either now or in the future because she had foolishly picked the wrong man to love and marry. That was her mistake and she would not allow her little boy or girl to pay the price of that mistake because it was a mistake that would reverberate down through the childhood years and leave a scar that wouldn't heal.

# CHAPTER NINE

NINE MONTHS AFTER Tia's disappearance, Max finished the last phone call and stared at his desk. The Reverend Mother had promised him she would get in touch if she heard anything from Tia and she had not. Inez Santos had snarled down the phone that she had still not heard from her daughter and had no desire to hear from her. Ronnie had never been in a position to offer him any helpful leads. Tia had not confided in anyone.

The trail, such as it was, was dead. Tia had departed in a taxi with one suitcase and Teddy. The taxi had taken her to the railway station from where she had travelled to London. A couple of weeks later there had been a possible sighting of her on a train heading to Devon. He supposed that he should at least be grateful that she had inherited her grandmother's money and was presumably making use of it. At least it meant that she was not destitute. But she had not once used the credit cards that he had given her or attempted to access the substantial private income that Andrew had set up for her. No, she had rejected everything Max and Andrew had given her and walked away.

Every line of the letter she had left behind haunted Max. It had been so blunt, so honest. *You don't really want me.* That said all that needed to be said in terms of his performance as a husband, didn't it? He had been married to Tia for over three months and that was the impression she had taken away from the experience. *You married me to please Andrew.* No, he hadn't but he needed to find her to tell her that. *You don't want to be a father.* Well, she had got that right. *You don't want our baby.* She had got that wrong. He had climbed aboard that man train where you acted strong rather than admit fear and ambiguity and he had shot himself in the foot. Tia didn't understand because he hadn't told her what she needed to know to understand. And now it was too late.

Max lifted his chin, his formidable bone structure grim. It would never be too late because he would not give up. When something truly mattered to him, he refused to accept defeat. Somehow, sooner or later, he would find some small piece of information that would lead him to his runaway bride and he would then face his biggest challenge—persuading her to come home. Her and Teddy and hopefully their child. Had she had a safe delivery?

But he reckoned bringing his little family home to Redbridge—if all had gone well—would be the toughest challenge he had ever faced. Tia, after all, had never truly wanted to marry him. She hadn't wanted to be tied down to a husband and if she had made the best of it for a few months he should be grateful for small mercies. She had wanted her freedom and now she had taken it. What nagged at Max most of all was the insidious suspicion that, had he moved more slowly with Tia, she would have wanted to stay married to him.

Tia tenderly zipped Sancha Mariana Leonelli back into her sleeping bag and tucked her back into her cot where she would sleep while her mother baked.

Motherhood was very different from what Tia had expected. She had not been remotely prepared for the intense joy that flooded her when she initially saw her infant daughter's little face or for the anxiety that rocked her when Sancha got her first cold. After three months of being a mum, however, she had become a little more laid-back but she could still get emotional. When Sancha opened the dark liquid eyes that she had inherited from her father along with his blue-black hair, Tia's heart clenched and her eyes sometimes stung because she was learning that time did not heal every pain.

Even nine months away from Max had failed to cure her heartache. Yet during those months of independence she had discovered so many enjoyable things and she had worked hard to make the days go past more quickly. But neither the satisfaction of a walk in sunlit frosted fields nor hard work had made her miss Max one atom less.

She had missed him worst of all when she gave birth to Sancha. Having attended a pre-natal class and made some friends, she had not been entirely alone at the hospital, but the absence of the man she loved had made her feel painfully isolated. Yet she knew that was ironic when Max had wanted neither her nor their child and would, had he but known it, have been very grateful to avoid the hullabaloo of childbirth and the chaotic aftermath of learning how to live with a newborn.

She had made friends when she moved to the picturesque village with the ancient church. In summer the village was busy with tourists. She had bought a little corner terraced house that came with an attached tea room, which she planned to open as a business in the spring. During the winter, she had baked traditional Brazilian cakes to offer at a church sale, and when the requests had come in for birthday cakes and fancy desserts she had fulfilled them and had ended up taking orders and eventually charging for the service. Before she knew where she was she was selling them like proverbial hotcakes and barely able to keep up with the demand.

Tia marvelled that a talent she had not even recognised as a talent was now providing her with a good living. She had learned to bake at Sister Mariana's side and the fabulous cakes she produced had once provided an evening treat at the convent. Her repertoire ran from coconut cake to passion fruit mousse cake and back to peach pound cake, which could be sliced and toasted for breakfast and served with fruit and cream. She planned to make her cakes the mainstay of her offerings at the tea room when it opened and, that in mind, she had hired a local woman to work with her.

Hilary was an energetic brunette and a terrific baker. Experienced in catering, she had helped Tia deal with suppliers and customers and had helped her work through the stringent health and safety regulations that had to be passed before the reopening of the tea shop could be achieved.

'Sancha is already sleeping through the night for you,' Hilary remarked enviously, the mother of a rumbustious boy, who was still disturbing her nights at three years old.

'And I am transformed,' Tia responded with a roll of her eyes. 'I was run pretty ragged the first couple of months. Just getting myself up in the morning was a challenge. I couldn't have done all this without you.'

'No, you couldn't have done it without your incredible cakes,' Hilary countered with a wry smile. 'Not many women could have achieved as much as you have in a few short months. Certainly not as a preggers mum-to-be on her own. Do you think your husband will eventually want to come and visit?'

'I don't know,' Tia said awkwardly, wishing that she had found it possible to lie to Hilary and pretend that Sancha was the result of a one-night stand. Instead she had found herself admitting that her marriage had broken down when she had revealed her pregnancy to a man who was less than keen on fatherhood. 'Tea?'

'Even if he wasn't that keen on being a dad, he's bound to be curious. I think you should consider giving him a chance,' Hilary reasoned, settling at the table with her tea and some paperwork. 'But then what do I know? I didn't do so well with my own marriage.'

Tia stared out of the window while she drank her own tea and brooded over the unsettling thoughts that Hilary had awakened. Sancha *was* Max's daughter as well. Had she given Max a fair chance in the parenting stakes? She knew she hadn't given him a chance at all. Despite his lack of enthusiasm over her pregnancy, wasn't there at least a possibility that his reservations would have melted away once he saw his baby daughter in the flesh? And just when was she planning to give him that chance?

Why was it that she hadn't thought about what was fair to Max nine months ago? She had made her deductions and acted on them in the heat of emotion, which was never wise. Everything had happened so fast: her marriage and her pregnancy, Andrew's death and his will and her unsettling encounter with her mother, when once again she had been forced to recognise that she was the child of a woman who chilled her. Would she still have walked out on Max if she had taken the time to think through events more calmly? Might she not have decided that talking to Max and giving him a fair hearing would be a more reasonable approach? More and more, Tia's conscience warned her that she had not so much walked out as run away from a situation that had made her feel trapped and powerless.

And whether she liked it or not, Sancha was Max's baby too. She had ignored his rights, favouring her own. And what about the divorce he probably wanted now? He would want his freedom back and the opportunity to move on with his life, but the vanishing act she had pulled would make that process even more difficult.

Tia was ashamed of the truth that she didn't want to give Max a divorce and see him move on to another woman. How could she be that selfish? Hadn't she walked away? He was entitled to his freedom if he wanted it. Not that he so far seemed to have taken much advantage of their separation, she conceded. Max had led quite an active life on the social scene before he met her, for she had checked him out on the Internet and, from what she had been able to establish since then, if Max *had* returned to his former lifestyle he was being very discreet about it. Of course, she had made that awkward for him too because he was neither single nor even officially separated from her.

And just as Tia had taken charge of her life nine months earlier she recognised that she had to come out of hiding now and face the music. It was time for her to stand up and deal with the challenges she had been avoiding. The very first step of that process, she acknowledged ruefully, would be contacting Max.

While Hilary was enjoying her tea, Tia pulled out her phone and before she could lose her nerve she accessed Max's phone number on her phone, attached a photo of Sancha to it and texted him her address as well as the name she had been using to avoid detection. For the sake of anonymity, she was known as Tia Ramos locally. Ramos had been her mother's maiden name.

Max received that text in the middle of a business meeting and his rage knew no bounds as he scrutinised his first blurry picture of his daughter, Sancha. She looked at the camera with big dark eyes, her tiny face astonishingly serious for a baby. Sancha Leonelli, Max was thinking in wonderment, until he read the full text message from his runaway wife and registered on a fresh tide of threatening fury that Tia had cast off the Leonelli name as entirely as she had cast off her husband. A blasted text! Not even a phone call. Was that all he rated after a nine-month silence? Nine months of unceasing worry that would have slaughtered a lesser man? A text… Max gritted his even white teeth, launched upright and strode out without even an apology for his departure. He had a wife to deal with.

Tia was slightly surprised when Max did not respond to her message. Had he changed his number?

Moved on from their marriage to the extent that he did not feel her text required an immediate response? Common sense kicked in, reminding her that Max had only just received his first glimpse of his baby daughter. More probably Max was furious with her. Anxiously mulling over those possibilities, Tia kept herself busy once she had put Sancha down for the night. The tea-room kitchen where she did all her baking was linked by a door to her house and, as long as she set up the baby monitor while she worked, she could hear her daughter if she wakened, but during the day she kept Sancha tucked in her travel cot and within easy reach.

She was busy packing an Anthill cake, which was stuffed with chocolate chips, when she heard her house doorbell ring and she sped back next door before the noise could waken Sancha. When she opened the door to Max she was knocked for six because the very last response she had expected from him was an instant unannounced visit.

'Oh, it's the kitchen fairy,' Max derided, running gleaming dark eyes down over her flour-smudged nose to her full ripe mouth and the shapeless chef's overall she wore. He had checked her out before his arrival and he knew all about the cakes she was baking. It irritated him that, not only had he not known that she could bake, but she had also not once made the effort to bake anything for him.

Tia went red, grateful she had removed her kitchen hat before she answered the door, but her fingers lifted to self-consciously smooth the hair braided neatly round her head. Poised below the porch light, Max looked amazing, blue-black hair glossy, his lean dark angel features smooth over his high cheekbones while a shadow of dark stubble roughened and accentuated the contrast between his angular jaw line and his wide, full modelled mouth. Her mouth ran dry.

'Or maybe it's Heidi and you're about to start yodelling,' Max breathed between gritted teeth.

'Heidi?' Tia frowned, not having come across that book as a child, staring up at him, frantically wishing she were dressed and wearing proper shoes with heels instead of clad for comfort and warmth in jeans, a winter sweater and flatties.

'It must be the cute little-girl braids,' Max extended sardonically, moving forward to force her to move back, a waft of cold air eddying into the house with him. 'Makes you look about ten years old.'

Tia backed several steps and thrust the door shut behind him. 'You should've told me you were coming,' she protested defensively, feeling menaced by the intimidating size of Max in the confined area of her small hallway.

'My apologies,' Max intoned softly. 'Your nine months of silence killed any manners I ever had stone dead.'

Tia's colour flared again because there wasn't much she could say to that in her own defence. She had speculated so many times about what seeing Max again would be like and now she was appreciating that she had got it wrong every time. She was all flustered, every sense on overdrive. She had forgotten his sheer physical impact on her, the heightened heart rate that dampened her skin, the challenge to breathe evenly, the surge of helpless excitement when she collided with his brilliant dark golden eyes. Feeling weak and uneasy with that least allowable sensation, she hastily thrust open the lounge door.

'I'm sorry I didn't get in touch sooner,' Tia murmured tautly. 'I didn't know what to say. I know that's no excuse but—'

'You're right. It's not an excuse. If it was I'd have first call on it,' Max sliced in without warning. 'I didn't know what to say when you told me that you were pregnant...and, *Dio mio*, haven't you made me pay for that lack of verbal dexterity?'

Wrong-footed once again, Tia clasped her hands together tightly in front of her. 'I didn't want my child to have an uncaring father.'

'On what grounds did you assume that I would be uncaring?' Max shot back at her. 'And where is my daughter? I want to see her.'

'She's asleep.' Tia swallowed hard, unaccustomed to being under attack by Max, feeling the novelty of that unexpected experience like a sudden blow, her skin turning clammy and cold.

Max planted himself expectantly back by the door into the hall. 'I can be very quiet,' he told her.

'Max, I—'

'I've waited months. I won't wait any longer,' Max informed her impatiently. 'When was she born?'

Tia gave him the date of their daughter's birth.

'Naturally I've been worried sick about you all this time,' Max pointed out curtly. 'I wondered if you were ill, whether you were in hospital, seeing a doctor regularly for check-ups… I even wondered if you could have lost the baby.'

'I'm sorry, I didn't think my silence through,' Tia countered stiltedly, mounting the narrow stairs and then stepping back from the doorway of Sancha's little bedroom to let him precede her, if anything grateful for the distraction from the hard questions he was shooting at her and the guilt he had awakened.

Max had believed his rage would ebb once he entered the house but being greeted by his wife as though everything were normal when it was as far from normal as it was possible to be had grated on him. Being forced to *ask* to see his own daughter didn't help and the suffocatingly small bedroom sent another biting surge of fury through him. As a child he had had so little. Now that he had a child of his own he wanted his child to have everything, and everything encompassed space and comfort and every material advantage he could provide. Now he stood in a small slot of a room only just big enough for a cot and a chest of drawers. It was clean, adequate but not sufficient to satisfy him.

'The courts take a very dim view of mothers who

deny fathers all right of access to their children,' he heard himself impart grimly.

The blood chilled in Tia's veins because what she heard was a threat. 'I thought I was doing the best thing for all of us when I left. I thought you didn't want her, didn't want the responsibility.'

'But I never said that, did I? Nor did I ever suggest that you terminate the pregnancy or indeed anything of that nature,' Max reminded her fiercely, finally approaching the cot with somewhat hesitant steps and looking down to see what he could of the sleeping baby. The light from the landing illuminated her little face, the sweet sweep of lashes on her flushed baby cheeks, the fullness of the little rosebud mouth she had definitely inherited from her mother. The sudden tightness in his chest forced Max to drag in a long, deep, steadying breath. Sancha was very small and the short tufts of her tousled dark hair stuck up comically in all directions while her tiny starfish hand lay relaxed against the mattress.

'She's…gorgeous.' Max almost whispered the word, what he had planned to say next flying back out of his head while he drank in his first glimpse of his daughter.

'She looks just like you,' Tia framed nervously, still reeling from that reference to the courts and parental rights because she knew what she had done and was bright enough to fear the consequences.

'What does it say on her birth certificate?' Max prompted tautly.

'Sancha Mariana Leonelli. I didn't know any of your family names so I couldn't include any,' Tia told him. 'And the sisters were the only family I ever knew.'

'I wouldn't have wanted my family names included,' Max admitted in a raw undertone, striding back to the door. 'There are no good memories there that I would want carried on into the next generation.'

Tia chewed uncertainly at her lower lip and then glanced at him at the top of the stairs, clashing involuntarily with glittering dark eyes of challenge. 'I kind of suspected that,' she confided.

'That's why I found it so challenging to imagine becoming a father,' Max revealed, clattering down the stairs, using the activity as cover to make himself force out that lowering admission of vulnerability. 'Actually I couldn't imagine it… I found the concept too frightening.'

'Oh… Max,' Tia whispered, her eyes burning with a sudden rush of moisture and regret. 'Why didn't you tell me that? I was nervous of becoming a mother too. I worried that I wouldn't be able to cope or that I wouldn't be able to feel attached to my baby because…for whatever reasons… Inez never got properly attached to me.'

'Even so, my background is considerably less presentable than yours,' Max volunteered diffidently. 'I have never discussed that reality with anyone, which only makes it more difficult for me to talk about it.

But my aunt didn't *want* to know and Andrew said my past was better left decently buried, so I kept my experiences to myself.'

Tia was aghast that a clearly damaged child had been forced to keep his ordeal a secret that decent people needed to be protected from. 'I don't think that was the right approach.'

'I don't know,' Max conceded with a grim shake of his arrogant dark head. 'Perhaps if I'd been encouraged to talk and think about what happened I would have wallowed in it, which would have been worse. I had nightmares at first and they still come occasionally.'

'I remember you dreaming,' Tia remarked uncomfortably.

Max nodded confirmation. 'But aside of that I did manage to move on without looking back, but my own experiences ensured that I had no plans to ever have kids. There's bad blood in me and I didn't want to pass it on—'

'There's no such thing as "bad blood",' Tia interrupted, angry on his behalf. 'Who used that expression?'

'My aunt. Carina was always waiting for me to reveal some violent, criminal tendency that I had inherited from my father. She never trusted me and never let me forget the fact.'

Seeing no point in sharing her poor opinion of his aunt's attitude towards the child in her care, Tia breathed in slow and deep. 'Your father was violent?'

'Very violent. An alcoholic tyrant. He didn't start out that way though. He was from a decent family and the son of a well-respected businessman but he became a drug-dealing thug at a young age. His family threw him out and he took up with my mother, who was equally wayward in her youth. She once told me that I was the child of his rape,' Max breathed curtly. 'But I suspect that that was her excuse for getting involved with a vicious loser. I'll never know because they are both dead now and the truth died with them.'

'Oh, Max,' Tia muttered, tormented on his behalf. 'What a truly awful thing to tell an innocent child.'

Max froze by the window, bold bronzed profile set, wide shoulders rigid. 'He killed her when I was twelve years old, during one of their frequent rows about money. I was there when it happened. He went to prison for life, which is why I ended up in England with my aunt. He died in prison a few years ago.'

And there was so much revealed in those few clipped sentences that Tia reeled, her every expectation trounced by his brutal honesty. She was very much shocked. He had seen his father murder his mother and had then become his aunt's responsibility. 'You must've been traumatised,' she framed shakily.

'Completely but I got over that and learned how to function in my new life,' Max countered briskly to discourage her sympathy. 'To be frank, that new life was one hell of a lot better than my old life. Plenty of food, a comfortable bed, no beatings, no police harassment, no bullying at school. It was a cakewalk compared with what I had been used to.'

'I'm so sorry, Max,' Tia breathed tautly. 'I had no idea.'

'How could you have had? It's not information I share and it's my past, not my present, Tia,' he declared with forbidding finality. 'I've only trailed all this out now so that I can try to explain to you why I was less than enthusiastic about the idea of becoming a father. There are no male role models in my background. My only role model came when I was older and it was Andrew, and even he turned out to be not quite the man I believed him to be. I was afraid that I'd be a useless father.'

'But you're not your father. You have none of his violence in you. Even tonight when you're so angry with me I have not once felt physically threatened by you,' she pointed out, wanting to ask him how her grandfather had disappointed him, but reluctant to demand too much at once from a man who was only telling what he had so far told her because he felt he had no other choice. 'You're also honourable and honest, responsible and law-abiding.'

'Yet my wife walked out on that honest, honourable, non-violent man and hid herself from me and stayed away as long as she could,' Max retorted with crushing dismissal. 'So, where does that leave us?'

Tia flinched from that sardonic reminder. 'That's a whole different story,' she argued in consternation.

'The leaving was about me, not you. I was so unsure and confused about everything in my life. Everything changed so fast and then Andrew died and you freaked out about me being pregnant—'

'I didn't freak out,' Max broke in angrily.

'In silence, you freaked out,' Tia rephrased. 'A first baby is a huge life change for a woman. I needed you to want our baby as much as I did because neither of us were wanted children and that didn't turn out well for us. I wanted our baby to have everything we didn't have, starting with caring, involved parents.'

'But you didn't give me a chance,' Max argued vehemently, dark eyes shimmering pure gold condemnation in the lamp light. 'Andrew had just died. I didn't want to lay my sordid background on you on top of everything else you were already going through. You were pregnant and I tried to deal with that as best I could without involving you.'

'Which meant you acted like it hadn't happened,' Tia slotted in ruefully. 'I couldn't handle that. We'd got married in a hurry. I'd got pregnant in a hurry. I had to put my child first and I knew I needed to be stronger. I couldn't get stronger *with* you because you were too busy looking after me to let me learn how to do things for myself. And I thought of Inez, who's spent her whole life needing a man to lean on and provide for her...and I was determined that *I* wasn't going to be that kind of weak woman.'

'Leaning on me isn't a weakness,' Max growled as the door bell sounded. 'Who's that?'

'Probably my customer wanting to pick up his party order,' Tia recalled belatedly. 'You stay here and I'll sort him out.'

But Max was too curious about the life that Tia had built away from him to keep his distance. He watched her greet a man in his thirties and walk through to a spacious catering kitchen to lift a set of cake boxes. Max's lean, strong face clenched as he listened to them banter like two old friends and he stepped back into the lounge while she showed her customer out again.

'Who is he?' he asked baldly when she reappeared. 'He was flirting with you.'

'Was he? I don't think so,' Tia responded with amusement to that suggestion because she had learned a thing or two over the past months. Now she knew when a man was flirting with her and when it was better to ignore an off-colour joke or call a halt to any overfamiliarity before someone got the wrong idea. 'He's a married man with five children and this is their third birthday party in as many months, so I've got to know him well.'

'How many other men have you got to know well?' Max enquired with lethal cool.

Tia glanced at him in open shock.

'Obviously I'm going to ask. I'd prefer honesty,' he admitted stonily.

Tia went pink. 'There hasn't been anyone...*anything*,' she breathed tightly. 'I'm very aware that I'm still married.'

'Ditto,' Max traded flatly. 'We've both been living in limbo since you walked out. If you wanted your freedom, Tia, you only had to say so. We could have separated with a lot less drama and stress.'

Tia lost colour. 'Is that what you want? A separation?'

Max settled glittering dark eyes on her. 'I'm still so angry with you that I don't know what I want.'

'Angry?' she queried uncertainly.

'Very angry,' Max qualified without hesitation. 'Perhaps you've forgotten that last night… I haven't.'

Tia's face flamed. In fact she felt as though her whole body were burning with mortification below her clothes.

'The last thing I was expecting the following morning was that letter. Why the goodbye sex?'

'I don't want to discuss that.'

Max planted himself in the doorway to prevent her from leaving the room. 'I'm afraid you're going to have to talk about a lot of stuff you don't want to talk about before I leave you alone. I deserve the truth, Tia. I have always tried to be straight with you.'

Tia spun away from him, embarrassment claiming her, for she had often squirmed when she looked back to the way she had wantonly thrown herself at him that night after the funeral. 'Oh, for goodness' sake, I wanted you… *OK?*' she exclaimed.

'The wanting was more than OK but the walking out on our marriage afterwards wasn't,' Max delivered icily. 'Not giving me the opportunity to answer your concerns was very unfair as well. There are no polite words to cover what I went through over the following months worrying about you. The press speculated that you'd left me because I screwed you over with your inheritance and they had a field day with your convent upbringing in comparison to my freewheeling days of sexual freedom.'

'I had no idea!' Tia exclaimed in dismay. 'I don't read many newspapers but I've kept a very low profile here. There was only that one photo of me that appeared in the papers, the one taken the night of the Grayson party and nobody would associate that designer-clad young woman with the woman I am now. I don't try to draw attention to myself here with my clothes or hair or anything.'

Max didn't know whether he should tell her that nothing could detract from the pure symmetry of her delicate features, the clarity of her skin or the slender suppleness of her body. 'But that simply means that you're living a lie here with Sancha,' he condemned.

Tia bridled, eyes widening, head flipping back. 'What's that supposed to mean?'

'That no matter what you do, you're a very wealthy heiress and my wife. You can't escape what you are, short of returning to Brazil and joining the good sisters again. This is your life and mine.'

An irritable burst of barking from outside made Tia unfreeze. 'Oh, I forgot about Teddy! I let him out into the garden while I was packing those cakes.'

Brushing past him, Tia sped out and seconds later Teddy surged into the room, freezing with a growl the instant he settled his eyes on the unexpected visitor and then moving closer to sniff at Max's trouser legs.

'You've met up with worse than me since we last were together?' Max conjectured, daring to reach down and pat Teddy's head. The terrier made no attempt to growl or bite.

'He's got much more used to other people, living here. I take him for regular walks.' Tia paced restlessly round the room, her full attention welded to Max's lean, powerful figure. 'Where do we go from here, Max?'

'You want an upfront list of demands?' Max queried. 'I want you to come home so that I can get to know my daughter.'

'Redbridge Hall is not my home,' Tia parried in disbelief.

'I may have been paying your staff for you for the past nine months but, legally and every other way, Redbridge is yours until you either sell it or dispose of it in some other way. And the will probably restricts what you *can* do because Andrew wanted the property kept in the family,' Max reminded her.

'*You've* been paying the staff?' Tia gasped.

'Well, someone had to take responsibility for them,' Max pointed out very drily. 'Your grandfather employed a lot of people and several businesses operate on the estate. I think eventually you will decide to scale down the household staff to a more appropriate level.'

Tia had lost all her natural colour. 'I didn't think.'

'No, of course you didn't. You've never had staff before but now that you do, you do have to take care of them. And there are decisions waiting that I was unable to deal with because I am *not* the legal owner of the estate,' he pointed out.

Tia reddened. 'I'm so sorry, Max. I should've thought of all that.'

'On the good news front, Grayson Industries is flourishing as never before and the profits will be astronomical this year because I've had little else but work to occupy me,' he proclaimed with sardonic bite.

Tia sank weakly down on an armchair. Of course, he wanted her back at Redbridge to release him from the added burden of what had never been his responsibility in the first place. She was ashamed that it had not even occurred to her that in her absence life had had to continue at Redbridge. Wages had to be paid, maintenance decisions made and probably requests had had to be answered because the estate land was often used for local events.

'I don't care about the profits,' she declared woodenly.

Max crouched down in front of her to study her with scorchingly furious dark golden eyes. 'Well, I and thousands of other people employed by Grayson's *do* care,' he countered with lethal derision. 'And it's *all* yours. I may be in charge, I may be the figurehead but at the end of the day all those profits are yours, *not* mine.'

Taken aback by his vehemence, Tia flinched back a few inches. 'But that's not what Andrew intended.'

Max swore long and low in Italian, literal sparks dancing in his stunning dark eyes. 'I don't care what Andrew intended. I will only take the salary and the bonus package that was agreed when I first took over. I will not live off my wife's wealth, or my ex-wife's…or whatever you are planning to become.'

Tia was more shaken still by that aggressive statement. Max vaulted upright again, long, lean muscles flexing in his thighs, the fabric of his trousers pulling taut. She recognised that he had run out of patience and that he wanted decisions now. But she was taken aback by his attitude to the Grayson wealth. He didn't want what he saw as *her* money.

'What do you want now, Max?' she murmured tautly. 'You haven't told me that yet.'

Max froze. The anger she had sent soaring through him ebbed and he thought about what *he* wanted. He looked at her and what he wanted was very, very basic. 'I want you to untangle your hair from those ties and strip. I want sex. It's been nine months and I've never gone through a dry spell this long since I grew up.'

Shock rocked Tia where she sat, transfixed like a deer in headlights. Slow colour rose in a tide below her fair skin, heat curling at the heart of her, touching and warming places she had stopped thinking about when she left him. She had suppressed that part of herself, her sensual side, meeting with it only in dreams that she could not control. Now she gazed back at Max, marvelling that he was so bold, so unapologetic about what he wanted and oddly excited by the forceful sexual energy he saw no reason to hide.

# CHAPTER TEN

'AND NOW THAT I've begun being honest, I'll continue in the same vein,' Max gritted in a driven undertone, working off a 'might as well be hung for a sheep as a lamb' soapbox. 'I also want my daughter with me under the same roof. I will not negotiate on that demand. I've missed out on an entire three months of her life and I'm a stranger to her through no fault of my own. That has to change—and fast. We'll return to Redbridge Hall tomorrow.'

'That's absolutely impossible!' Tia exclaimed, leaping upright in emphasis, guilt, shock and consternation flooding her in a heady tide. 'I'm about to open the tea room for the Easter visitors and I have loads of orders to fulfil.'

'You also have a very competent co-worker and you can afford to hire another employee to take your place. Oh, yes, I did my homework before I came here,' Max intoned with sizzling cool.

'But you don't understand... Salsa Cakes is *my* business.'

'No, your business is Grayson Industries,' Max contradicted without hesitation. 'Not what you have here. It's time to join the real world again, Tia. You were born into one of the richest families in the UK and you can't run away from your heritage.'

'I didn't run away!' Tia seethed back at him, her hands clenched into fists by her sides, her colour high.

'Your choice, your decision. I'm sorry but you're rich and you're married to a bastard who will take you any way he can get you. Deal with it, *bella mia… I have.*'

The thready wail of a hungry baby pierced the smouldering silence and very quickly grew into a much louder demonstration of baby impatience. 'I'd better feed Sancha,' Tia mumbled, bereft of breath and protest, indeed barely able to think or vocalise, too shaken by the change in Max, who certainly could not be accused of soft-coating his message.

She ran upstairs to scoop her daughter out of her cot and returned to the lounge at a slower pace. As Max moved forward, his lean, darkly handsome features unexpectedly softened, she disconcerted him by literally stuffing her sobbing child into his surprised arms. 'Max, meet Sancha… Sancha, this is Daddy and he is at the very foot of a learning curve when it comes to babies.'

'But I'm a quick study,' Max asserted, bundling up Sancha and resting her against his shoulder, a big hand smoothing her back in a soothing motion.

'I have to heat her bottle…and…er…change her…'

'You don't breastfeed?'

'I did initially but I had problems so we ended up with the bottle and she's thriving,' Tia explained, leaving him to go and take care of necessities.

Max sat down and surveyed his angry-eyed daughter, who was struggling to catch her breath between sobs. He extracted her from the sleeping bag with great care and was amazed by how wriggly her fragile, light little body was. He was surprised to realise that much of his own anger had dissipated. Telling Tia how he felt had helped. Holding his daughter helped even more. All of a sudden he realised that he had moved on from the past that had once haunted him. Sharing that background story had been like curing an illness he had kept locked up inside him. And now he was looking forward and not back on a successful adult life, a stunning wife and an equally beautiful daughter.

My *daughter,* Max thought in wonderment, studying the little being snug in his arms. Her eyes and hair might be dark like his own but the shape of her eyes, her mouth and possibly her little button nose were all her mother's. Her very beautiful mother. Max breathed in deep, fighting the reaction of his body with all his strength. He had been crude but the truth was the truth. All the months without Tia had suddenly just piled up in the back of his brain like a giant rock crushing him. Life without Tia was dull, predictable and barely worth living.

*A bastard who will take you any way he can get you.*

Tia had been shaken by that statement but strangely fired up by his raw conviction as well. Max *was* very likely illegitimate, she acknowledged, for the background he had described seemed unlikely to have contained legally wedded parents. Why on earth was she thinking about something so irrelevant when Max had laid down what he wanted and it was *all*—from the sex to the immediate relocation—unacceptable?

The trouble was...life without Max was equally unacceptable because she wasn't happy. That was a huge admission for Tia to make to herself when she had worked so hard to achieve independence. She adored her baby, she loved her little house and her embryo business, but existing deprived of Max's presence was like eating curry every day without the spice. Nothing else could compare to the joy of knowing Max was in the room next door, within reach and with their daughter. Even though he was angry, knowing Max was near her again was like her every fantasy come true, she acknowledged shamefacedly. She still loved him. She hadn't got over him. She looked at him and the wanting kicked in again within seconds and it was like coming alive after a long stretch of being denied sunshine and stimulation. Could she settle for the wanting? It did seem to be *all* Max had to give her.

'I'll show you how to feed her.' Tia slotted the bottle into his lean brown hand and showed him the angle. 'She guzzles it down quickly at this time of night.'

And Max settled back into a more relaxed pose and fed their child and the sight of them together warmed the cold space inside Tia, because she had feared that her baby would never have a proper father and that that was entirely her fault. Max followed her upstairs and watched her settle Sancha again.

'You said something about my grandfather not being the man you thought he was,' she reminded him softly. 'What was that about?'

Max groaned. 'I shouldn't have mentioned it.'

'Whatever it is, tell me. I'm sure Andrew wasn't a saint all his life. Nobody is,' she said wryly.

'Did you notice the interest at the dining table on the night you first arrived when you mentioned my aunt's death?' Max prompted.

'Yes, I did,' Tia admitted.

'When I was in my teens, I came back to Redbridge from school unannounced one day and saw Andrew and my aunt kissing. I was shocked,' Max confided. 'Shocked and embarrassed. It was never discussed but I picked up on the evidence after that and realised they'd been having an affair for years.'

'Never...discussed... I mean, even after she died?' Tia pressed in disbelief.

'Never,' Max confirmed. 'I don't think it was any great love affair. I think it was two lonely people finding comfort in each other. Andrew was depressed for a long time after his wife passed away and, although he and my aunt were very discreet, a lot of the family knew about their relationship and regarded her as his mistress.'

Tia wrinkled her nose with distaste. 'That must have been awkward for you.'

Max shrugged. 'I was used to stuff that is whispered behind backs and never openly declared. When I lived in Italy my parents were despised for their lifestyle and I was despised too. Secrets were familiar to me as well. I was also intelligent enough to realise that Andrew probably paid for my fancy boarding school education because an adolescent hanging around on a daily basis would have cramped their style. But I can't complain because I benefitted from that education.'

'I'm surprised he didn't marry her.'

'Marrying his housekeeper wouldn't have been Andrew's style,' Max opined wryly.

On the landing, Tia turned in an unsettled half-circle. 'I assume you're planning to stay here tonight.'

'Yes. I have an overnight bag in my car. I'll bring it in.'

As it was a two-bedroom house with only one small double bed in her room, an involuntary tingle that was far removed from panic shimmied through Tia. What was she playing at? What was she planning to do? Obviously she had to return to Redbridge Hall and deal with matters there, whether she was making arrangements for the house in the short term or more lasting plans for the future. That was, undeniably, her responsibility.

More importantly, Max was demanding full access to Sancha and she could hardly criticise him for that. Their daughter would benefit from a normal relationship with her father. And Tia, who didn't want to picture a future empty of Max, wanted that as well.

'Is there a shower I can use?' Returned to the present, Tia showed Max the bathroom, which was perfectly presentable because she had had to have it replaced soon after moving in.

He had *arrived* with an overnight bag. The significance of that when there was little accommodation to rent in the village outside the tourist season made Tia's lips quirk. Max had never planned to take no for an answer. Max had come prepared with an ultimatum.

*He would take her any way he could get her.*

Which was pretty much the same as he had said the day of the funeral.

*Somehow in a very short space of time you became both the icing* and *the cake... I'm possessive.*

Caveman-speak for love? Whatever he felt for her, time hadn't changed him in the essentials and she was suddenly awesomely grateful for that reality. He didn't have a collection of sweet words or compliments to offer her but he was very honest and she loved him for that quality.

As Max emerged from the bathroom, his shirt loose and unbuttoned to display a slice of bronzed chest, Tia slid past him, clad in a robe, and stepped straight into the shower. He was right: she *had* run away from Redbridge, using the belief that he didn't want their child as an excuse. But she had needed that breathing space, that time alone to be independent and self-sufficient so that she could think for herself and finish growing up. She knew now that she *could* live her dream but that her dream would not be perfect in the starry way she had imagined it. And in truth she no longer wanted that original dream if it didn't contain Max. Most probably she did not figure in any of Max's dreams, but perhaps she would have to settle for that because half a loaf was better than no bread at all, particularly when it meant she could live with the man she loved and give her daughter the father she deserved.

Tia brushed her hair. It rippled in snaking waves across her shoulders, volumised by the braiding she used to confine it every day. Her heart beating very fast, Tia walked back into the bedroom.

'You're not allowed in the bed,' Max was telling Teddy grimly as he tried to stop the terrier from tunnelling under the duvet to take up his favourite position.

'He's a great foot warmer on a cold night.'

'No,' Max told her forcefully as he straightened, a lithe bronzed figure clad only in silk boxers, his muscular abs rippling with his movement.

Tia's breath escaped in a faint hiss as she averted her eyes and scooped Teddy off the bed to stow him in his basket. 'He can be very pushy. He'll just wait until we're asleep and sneak back in,' she warned him.

Max slid back into the bed while she watched dry-mouthed, as impressionable as a teenager with a first crush. His biceps flexed as he tossed the duvet back out of her way and looked expectantly at her. One glance and he froze. Honey-blonde swathes of hair foamed round her heart-shaped face, framing her mesmerising blue eyes and soft, full mouth. She shed the robe to reveal a vest top and shorts with a cutesy dog print. He breathed in slow and deep to restrain himself but he still wanted to grab her and fall on her like a hungry, sex-starved wolf.

'Why did you pack an overnight bag?' Tia murmured. 'How did you know you'd be staying?'

'I knew I couldn't risk leaving you once I actually

found you. It would be too easy for you to disappear again,' Max breathed curtly.

Tia looked at him in astonishment. 'But I bought this place. I couldn't just pull up sticks and walk out of here on a whim.'

'You did before and you have the resources to stage a vanishing act any time you want,' he reminded her. 'I won't risk losing you and my daughter again.'

Shame gripped Tia as she scrambled below the duvet. 'I wouldn't do that to you again.'

Blonde hair brushed his arm and she turned over to look at him, cornflower-blue eyes full of regret. 'I promise I won't leave like that ever again.'

Max's gaze dropped to her soft, full mouth and he tensed, dense black lashes lifting on burning golden eyes, fierce sexual energy leaping through him in a stormy surge. The chemistry got in the way of his brain, he finally acknowledged. That intense pull had clouded his judgement from the first moment he saw her. He was determined not to let it happen again.

Tia lifted a hand that felt detached from her control and stroked her forefinger very gently along the sensual curve of his lower lip and she shivered, hips squirming, the heat at the heart of her making her press her thighs together for relief. Max stared down at her and the silence throbbed and pulsed, the atmosphere so tense it screamed at her.

And then he took the bait that she had only dimly recognised was bait and his mouth came down so hard on hers she couldn't breathe. His lips pushed hers apart and his tongue delved and her spine arched and all of a sudden she couldn't speak because her body was doing the talking for her, lifting up into the hard, muscular strength of his, legs splaying, breasts peaking. A powerful hunger was unleashed in both of them and it swept them away. He came down on her, flattening her to the bed, crushing her breasts, and he kissed her until her mouth was swollen and reddened.

'You want this…?' he husked, giving her that choice at the last possible moment.

'Want…*you*,' Tia protested, her back bowing and her legs rising and locking round his lean hips as he pushed into her yielding flesh with a hungry groan of need.

And it was wild and rough and passionate and exactly what they both needed, a release from the shocking tension that had built throughout the evening. Afterwards, Tia lay slumped in Max's arms, utterly drained but happy.

Max was already wondering if he had got it wrong again, feeling like a man who had a very delicate glass ornament in his hand and who had accidentally damaged it. He never knew what to do with Tia; he never knew what to say to her. What he did say when he was striving to be honest tended to come out wrong, so he knew that his silence was a necessary precaution. Even so, the knowledge that he would wake up with her in the morning brought a flashing smile of relief to his lips. She had both arms wrapped around him and he decided he liked it. Teddy regarded him balefully from his basket but nothing could dull Max's mood.

Max knew nothing about love. He hadn't grown up with that example to follow, Tia was musing, and the one time he had surrendered to that attachment he had been deceived and hurt. But she knew as sure as God made little apples that the look in Max's eyes when he'd first held Sancha had been the onset of love. If he could love their daughter, he could learn how to love Tia. Baby steps, she told herself soothingly, baby steps.

Max woke up in the morning with his wife and a terrier. Said terrier had sneaked into the bed during the night and, far from settling in the location of a foot-warmer, had instead imposed himself between Max and Tia like a doggy chastity belt. Max's phone was buzzing like an angry bee and his daughter was crying and he eased out of bed, leaving Tia soundly asleep.

He was thrilled with his achievement when he contrived to make up a bottle for Sancha by following the very precise instructions. He gave Teddy a large slice of cake, which hugely boosted his standing in the dog's eyes, and Teddy stationed himself protectively at his feet while he fed his daughter. That done, he carried the little girl back upstairs to find clean clothes for her. Changing her and dressing her was the biggest challenge he had ever met because she wouldn't stay still and her legs and arms got lost in the all-in-one garment he finally got her dressed in. But she was clean and warm and that was all that mattered, he told himself while he made arrangements on his phone to have Tia's possessions moved to Redbridge Hall.

Tia came racing downstairs in a panic when she found Sancha missing from her cot, and Max looked forgivably smug when she stared in surprise at her daughter slumbering peacefully in her travel cot, utterly lost in an outfit at least two sizes too large for her.

'You should've wakened me,' she told him in discomfiture.

'No. I want to be involved whenever I can be.' Gleaming dark golden eyes locked to her, Max slid upright and stretched indolently, long sleek muscles flexing below his shirt as he reached for his jacket. 'You need to see that we can do this better together and that I can be as committed to Sancha as you are. I don't plan to work eighteen-hour days any more, not now I have both of you back in my life. That is a fair assumption, isn't it?' he pressed tautly. 'You are...*back*?'

'Yes, I'm back,' Tia murmured, torn up inside by

the sudden flash of insecurity she read in his strained gaze. He wasn't sure of her yet, didn't quite trust that she would go the distance, and she didn't think she could blame him for that.

It was two days before they got away from her house, two days of frantic packing and planning with Hilary, who would manage Salsa Cakes and in due course open the tea room with Tia's financial backing. Max made himself very useful thrashing out the business details.

Late season snow was falling softly as they drew up outside Redbridge Hall. The trees were frosted white and the air was icy cold. When Tia walked into the spacious hall where a fire was burning merrily in the grate, she felt as if she was coming home for the first time.

'It's our first wedding anniversary,' Max reminded her with satisfaction.

'My goodness, is it?' Tia exclaimed, mortified that she had forgotten.

'I'm afraid that because I didn't know you would be here I haven't made any special preparations.'

'That's OK. Just us being here together is enough,' Tia whispered as they went upstairs with Janette, the housekeeper, to see the room that had been prepared for their daughter.

'It'll need decorating,' Max grumbled.

'It's perfect,' Tia insisted, able to see how much work the staff had put in trying to make an adult bedroom look suitable for a baby. A very large and handsome antique cot had been refurbished with a new mattress and, laid on it, Sancha looked little bigger than a doll. Tia rummaged through her bags of baby essentials until she had located everything she needed to make her daughter feel comfortable.

'We should hire a nanny to help out,' Max suggested. 'We stayed home every evening while Andrew was ill becausc we didn't want to leave him alone but I'd like to get back to having a social life and sometimes you'll be staying in my London apartment. We need that extra flexibility.'

Tia nodded thoughtfully. While she couldn't imagine having a nanny, she did want to spend as much time as possible with Max. The life they had led during the first months of their marriage had been limited by her grandfather's infirmity and they had rarely gone out.

Max dropped a hand to her spine and walked her into their bedroom. 'I had this room updated. It was dark and dreary before.'

'But very grand,' she conceded, scanning the lighter colour scheme with approval. 'This is an improvement.'

'I do have one gift for you,' Max murmured, indicating the wrapped package on the bed.

Tia smiled and began to rip the fancy paper off to expose an exceptionally pretty framed picture.

'It's the Grayson family tree,' Max murmured. 'I

thought you would enjoy seeing exactly where you come from and who your forebears were.'

The names had been done in exquisite calligraphy, and hand-painted flowers decorated the borders. It was a thoughtful, meaningful gift and her heart turned over inside her because the information on her own family tree was exactly the kind of information she had been denied all her life when her father had insisted that her curiosity was foolish because she would never even travel to England.

'It's really beautiful, Max. Thank you,' she whispered sincerely. 'This means a lot to me. I like what you've had done to this room as well.'

'I haven't used it since you left. I came back here every weekend. It gave the staff a reason for being here.'

Tia studied his lean, strong face. 'I haven't thanked you for that yet…for looking after things for me.'

'That's my job. That's what I do. All my working life I have taken care of stuff for other people…their money, their businesses. But when it's for you, it's a little bit more special and it doesn't feel like work,' Max volunteered.

'Why is that…do you think?' Tia prompted hopefully.

Max glanced at her in surprise. 'You're my wife and this is your home.'

'This is *your* home too,' Tia reminded him. 'When

we got married I had nothing and you're not the housekeeper's nephew any more. You're the man Andrew chose to run Grayson Industries and the man he asked to marry me.'

'No regrets there,' Max breathed. 'Not now I've got you back again.'

'You honestly don't regret marrying me?'

'How could I regret it? There is some stuff I regret,' Max admitted reluctantly, his lean, darkly handsome face grave. 'Mainly that I had to rush you into marriage, but I hate that I missed out on you being pregnant and that I wasn't by your side when you had Sancha.'

'I thought you'd be very uncomfortable with all that,' she confided.

'Why would I be when you were carrying our child?' Max asked simply. 'Maybe some day you'll consider having another baby and we'll share everything then right from the start.'

'Maybe in a year or so… I think I would find it all a lot less scary with you by my side,' Tia admitted, touched by the source of his regret and his evident hope that they would have another child. 'You know, it may not seem like it but… I love you very much, Max.'

'You already know how I feel about you and it didn't keep you *with* me, *amata mia*,' Max murmured in a roughened undertone.

'What do you mean, I already know?' Tia asked in bewilderment.

'I told you the day of the funeral that there would never be another woman for me, that you were "it" for me, as it were,' he completed very awkwardly.

'You said I was the icing and the cake,' Tia recalled abstractedly, totally thrown by what he was saying. 'Did you mean that you had fallen in love with me?'

'What else would I mean by that?' Max demanded, as if she were the one with faulty understanding. '*Dio mio*, I admitted that I couldn't stand the thought of losing you, that I didn't want any other man to have even a chance to take you from me. What else would I have meant?'

Tia gave him a tearful appraisal. 'I didn't get it... don't you understand? If I'd known you loved me, I would never have left. I thought you were talking about sex.'

'The sex is spectacular but nothing is as spectacular as just having you in my life, having you to come home to and having you smile at me. Are you sincerely saying that you wouldn't have left if I'd used the word "love"? I gave you a pendant with a diamond for every day we'd been married. Didn't that say it for me? Surely it was obvious how I felt?' Max was studying her with rampant incredulity. 'I could feel you slipping away from me that week. I was panicking and then the will was read and Andrew had stabbed me in the back and made everything impossible.'

A sob convulsed Tia's throat. 'Oh, Max, I don't care about the money. I *never* cared about the money. I don't even know what to do with it or how to take care of Grayson Industries. All I ever wanted was you and I've spent months breaking my heart for you and trying to have a life without you…and I hated my life without you! But I wouldn't admit that even to myself.'

'Tia… Tia…' Max framed her distressed face with trembling hands. 'It was love at first sight for me. I had no control over my feelings. I wanted you at any cost but I felt like a bastard for taking you to bed so quickly and then pushing you into a marriage you weren't really ready for. There is nothing I wouldn't do to make you happy and persuade you to stay with me. I need you.'

'I need you too,' Tia said chokily and flung herself into his arms. 'Love at first sight and you never even mentioned it!'

'I don't talk about stuff like that. You'd have thought I was mentally unstable if I'd told you at the time because we hardly knew each other,' Max argued vehemently.

'Then I was mentally unstable too!' Tia told him, covering his disconcerted face with kisses. 'I felt the same. Max… Max, I love you to the moon and back.'

'Loved you through all nine miserable months of

your absence,' Max confessed grittily. 'Thought… just my luck to fall for a bolter.'

'I swear that I will never leave you again!' Tia told him passionately as he settled her down on the bed while Teddy scratched unavailingly at the door.

'You love me…and yet you *still* left me,' Max marvelled in bewilderment. 'How is that possible?'

'I wanted our baby to have a loving father and I didn't think you wanted to be one. I also thought that possibly you felt trapped, getting married at Andrew's instigation and then me falling pregnant immediately.'

'I wouldn't have married you if I hadn't fallen for you like a ton of bricks. I knew what Andrew wanted but I'm my own man and I make my own decisions… and then I met this incredible Brazilian angel…well, angel-like,' Max adjusted as she wrestled him out of his jacket. 'And the writing was on the wall from that moment. One look and you owned me body and soul. One look and I knew I'd never want another woman again.'

'But you didn't show it and you didn't say it either,' Tia lamented. 'You've got to say the words for a woman to hear.'

Max said it in Italian because she startled him by ripping his shirt open.

'No, I don't know Italian. Say it in English,' she urged.

'You've come over all bossy,' Max commented warily.

'Please say it…' Tia urged, stroking a long muscular thigh encouragingly.

'I love you.' Max kept on saying it because the reward was Tia's full attention and her desire to incessantly touch him where he was very keen to be touched. 'But I didn't recognise that what I felt was love until it was too late.'

Teddy slept outside their bedroom door that night because his humans didn't emerge. The next night he sneaked in and slept under the bed until his snoring alerted Max to his presence and he got thrown out in the early hours. The third night he sat outside the door crying and gained entry by taxing Max's patience. He was satisfied with that advance in his campaign but his ambition was set on regaining his rightful place back in the bed and he was a very determined little dog.

Two and a half years later, Tia studied the traditional Brazilian Christmas cake she had baked for Max. It was his favourite and that was saying something because he liked all her cakes. She had started up another branch of Salsa Cakes at Redbridge and it was thriving and providing more employment on the estate. Her cousin, Ronnie, had become her closest friend and, keen to have a job now that her children were all at school, she did the accounts for Salsa Cakes.

Tia was always very busy, but then she liked to be busy if she could take time off when she needed it to be with Max. And now that they had a wonderful nanny, time off was no longer a problem. She had done a part-time course on estate management to help her to run Redbridge but she had taken up other interests as well. She raised funds for the convent orphanage and did community work at various charitable events and, with Max as an advisor, had set up a workshop at the settlement for handicrafts and toiletries made from Amazonian plants. The convent was thriving and she made regular visits back to her former home. As a rule, she and Max ended those trips with a self-indulgent few days relaxing in Rio.

In a few weeks, her mother, Inez, was marrying for the third time and Tia was attending the wedding. She was looking forward to spending some time with her two half-brothers and her half-sister. Inez had finally agreed to tell her children about Tia's existence and that had considerably enhanced Tia's attitude to her mother. Since then she had met her mother's second family on several occasions and they all got on well. As for her mother, well, she knew she was never going to be close to the older woman for they had nothing in common but at least they were now on relaxed and friendly terms.

Of course, Tia already had her own snug little

family with Max and Sancha. Sancha was a lively toddler on the brink of starting nursery school and Tia had decided that it was finally time to think of having another child. A baby was now on the way, the well-defined bump of her pregnancy reminding Tia of that fact every time she bent over a table and found her stomach was in the way. The new addition to the family would arrive in the new year. Max was very excited. He said there was more of her to hold and he seemed to like that. In fact, Tia thought cheerfully, Max seemed to relish every change that signified her advancing pregnancy. Where she saw fat, Max saw voluptuousness and he couldn't keep his hands off her.

Not that that was anything new in their marriage, Tia reflected with a heightening of colour in her cheeks. Sometimes she wondered if it was because they had come so close to losing each other that they never dared to forget how lucky they were to be together. And these days she could think without the smallest resentment that her grandfather had picked a very fine husband for her. Max was a terrific father, a great husband and a real family man, which was a wonderful trait to find in a male who had never enjoyed a proper family of his own.

The past no longer bothered Max. He had moved on from his sense of secret shame, learning that he could be whatever he wanted to be if he worked hard enough at it. He had set up an executive team to help him run Grayson Industries and was no longer so constantly on call. Unlike his mentor, Andrew, who had never spent much time with his two sons and whose relationship with them had suffered accordingly, Max put family first and work second.

It was Christmas Eve and Tia twitched the nativity scene in the hall into place with care. She had incorporated some Brazilian traditions into their Christmases. Now she sat down by the fire to await Max's return, Teddy at her feet and Sancha pretending to read very importantly from one of her picture books.

Max breezed through the front door festooned with packages. Sancha dived at him, telling him about her day while Teddy bounced at his feet, joining in the excitement but not actually greeting Max. Max smiled at her, his wide charismatic smile that never failed to light her up like a firework inside. Her beautiful Max.

'You look…amazing,' Max told her truthfully, because she did and he could never quite believe that she was his, his to hold and keep. In a black stretchy dress that hugged her shapely form, blonde hair bouncing on her slim shoulders, cornflower eyes sparkling, she took his breath away.

There was no end to the advantages of being married to Tia, Max thought complacently. There were the cakes, cakes to die for. There was Sancha and a second child on the way. There was the sheer joy of living with Tia's sunny, positive nature and her boundless energy. Sometimes he couldn't credit that one woman could transform his life as much as she had and he was tempted to pinch himself to be certain he hadn't dreamt his perfect woman up. There was something wonderfully reassuring about the arms Tia wrapped round him while the enthusiasm of her response to his kiss travelled straight to another spot.

Max surfaced abstractedly from that kiss to see their nanny taking Sancha off for her tea and Tia clasped her hand in his and led him up the stairs. 'I thought we were having Christmas cake,' he said weakly.

'After supper,' his wife told him repressively. 'We're on a timetable. We're going to Midnight Mass later.'

'And after…?' Max ran glittering dark golden eyes over her lovely face and exhaled with pleasurable anticipation. 'I love you, Mrs Leonelli…even when you dictate when I can eat cake.'

'The rules are for Sancha. You can eat cake whenever you like.'

'Only if I can bring it up to the bedroom with us. Teddy will take care of any crumbs,' Max bargained.

But Teddy wasn't falling for that unlikely offer. He knew Max wasn't a messy eater. Teddy's beady eyes were locked to the currently untended cake on the low coffee table.

Tia laughed and tasted Max's mouth again, sinuously, sensually, revelling in the knowledge of his arousal. He scooped her up into his arms on the landing, pretended to stagger at her increased weight, got mock-slapped for his teasing and totally forgot about his craving for cake. Tia told him how much she loved him and it all got very soppy, and then sexy, and then soppy again.

Teddy got the cake.

Tia got more diamonds for Christmas.

And a couple of months later a little boy was born and christened Andrew.

* * * * *

Available October 17, 2017

## #3569 THE ITALIAN'S CHRISTMAS SECRET

*One Night With Consequences*

by Sharon Kendrick

When chauffeur Keira Ryan drives into a snowdrift, she and Matteo Valenti must find a hotel—where they end up spending one sizzling night! It's Christmastime again before Matteo uncovers Keira's secret. Now it's time to claim his heir...

## #3570 A DIAMOND FOR THE SHEIKH'S MISTRESS

*Rulers of the Desert*

by Abby Green

Hiring model Kat is the perfect opportunity for Sheikh Zafir Al-Noury to resume their burning-hot nights. Once again, Zafir tempts Kat to sensual surrender. Even if that means exposing every part of herself to the man who once ruled her soul...

## #3571 THE SULTAN DEMANDS HIS HEIR

by Maya Blake

Esme Scott strikes a deal with Sultan Zaid to free her con-man father—but as his captive, she cannot deny their insatiable longing! A heated encounter leaves her pregnant... Zaid's sensual power soon persuades her to become a sultan's wife!

## #3572 CLAIMING HIS SCANDALOUS LOVE-CHILD

*Mistress to Wife*

by Julia James

Eloise Dean was innocent until she met Vito Viscari... Duty forced Vito to end their scorching nights, but months later he cannot resist returning to her. Then he discovers the shocking truth: Eloise is pregnant with his love-child!

HPCNM1017RA

## #3573 THE GREEK'S FORBIDDEN PRINCESS

*The Princess Seductions*

by Annie West

Tragedy brings the press swarming around Princess Amelie, so she takes her nephew and runs to Lambis Evangelos for protection. His desire for Amelie is incredible, but he's always refused to taint her. Until Amelie's forbidden temptation arrives at his doorstep...

## #3574 VALDEZ'S BARTERED BRIDE

*Convenient Christmas Brides*

by Rachael Thomas

The only way for Lydia to absolve her father's horrifying debts is to accept Raul Valdez's outrageous proposition. She must help him claim his inheritance—or marry Raul on Christmas Eve! Lydia finds she cannot resist her desire for the dark-hearted billionaire...!

## #3575 KIDNAPPED FOR THE TYCOON'S BABY

*Secret Heirs of Billionaires*

by Louise Fuller

Nola Mason doesn't expect to see Ramsay Walker again after their explosive fling, never considering the consequences! Ram must claim his heir—he'll steal her away to his rain-forest hideaway and use their heat-fuelled passion to entice her into marriage!

## #3576 A NIGHT, A CONSEQUENCE, A VOW

*Ruthless Billionaire Brothers*

by Angela Bissell

Emily Royce needs Ramon de la Vega's investment to save her business. But Ramon's piercing gaze reveals their potent chemistry—and one glorious night in Paris results in pregnancy! Ramon will make her his any way he can. Even with his ring!

---

*When chauffeur Keira Ryan drives into a snowdrift, she and her devastatingly attractive passenger must find a hotel… but there's only one bed! Luckily, Matteo Valenti knows how to make the best of a bad situation—with the most sizzling experience of her life. It's nearly Christmas again before Matteo uncovers Keira's secret. He's avoided commitment his whole life, but now it's time to claim his heir…*

*Read on for a sneak preview of*
Sharon Kendrick*'s book*
*THE ITALIAN'S CHRISTMAS SECRET*

One Night With Consequences

"Santino?" Matteo repeated, wondering if he'd misheard her. He stared at her, his brow creased in a frown. "You gave him an Italian name?"

"Yes."

"Why?"

"Because when I looked at him—" Keira's voice faltered as she scraped her fingers back through her hair and turned those big sapphire eyes on him "—I knew I could call him nothing else but an Italian name."

"Even though you sought to deny him his heritage and kept his birth hidden from me?"

She swallowed. "You made it very clear that you never wanted to see me again, Matteo."

His voice grew hard. "I haven't come here to argue the rights and wrongs of your secrecy. I've come to see my son."

It was a demand Keira couldn't ignore. She'd seen the brief tightening of his face when she'd mentioned his child and another wave of guilt had washed over her.

HPEXP1017

"Come with me," she said huskily.

He followed her up the narrow staircase and Keira was acutely aware of his presence behind her. She could detect the heat from his body and the subtle sandalwood that was all his and, stupidly, she remembered the way that scent had clung to her skin the morning after he'd made love to her. Her heart was thundering by the time they reached the room she shared with Santino and she held her breath as Matteo stood frozen for a moment before moving soundlessly toward the crib.

"Matteo?" she said.

Matteo didn't answer. Not then. He wasn't sure he trusted himself to speak because his thoughts were in such disarray. He stared down at the dark fringe of eyelashes that curved on the infant's olive-hued cheeks and the shock of black hair. Tiny hands were curled into two tiny fists and he found himself leaning forward to count all the fingers, nodding his head with satisfaction as he registered each one.

He swallowed.

His *son.*

He opened his mouth to speak but Santino chose that moment to start to whimper and Keira bent over the crib to scoop him up. "Would you…would you like to hold him?"

"Not now," he said abruptly. "There isn't time. You need to pack your things while I call ahead and prepare for your arrival in Italy."

"What?"

"You heard me. You can't put out a call for help and then ignore help when it comes. You telephoned me and now you must accept the consequences," he added grimly.

**Next month, Harlequin Presents welcomes you to the passionate world of Abby Green's new duet—Rulers of the Desert! Powerful monarchs Zafir and Salim have never had their wishes challenged—until they meet the women they're determined to take to their beds. Kat and Charlotte might find their seduction to be irresistible… But to claim them truly, their seducers must make them their desert queens!**

Sheikh Zafir Al-Noury cannot forgive model Kat Winters for breaking off their engagement—but neither can he forget their burning-hot nights together. Hiring her to promote his kingdom's most famous jewel creates an opportunity for renewed seduction…

Walking away from Zafir devastated Kat. The pain has made her strong, but the fire he ignites is stronger yet—Zafir tempts her to complete sensual surrender! Even if that means exposing every part of herself to the man who once ruled her soul…

***A Diamond for the Sheikh's Mistress***

Available now

***A Christmas Bride for the King***

Coming soon

HPBPA1017